THE MAN WHO TAMED LONE PINE

When Nathaniel McBain and Shackleton Frost arrive in Lone Pine to escort a prisoner to Beaver Ridge jail, they are shocked to discover it is Shackleton's old friend Sheriff Ashton Clarke. Five years ago, Ashton tamed the town, but now he's been charged with killing in cold blood. Ashton claims that someone from his past has framed him, and Shackleton believes his friend. But as more bodies are found, all the evidence points to Ashton, and the case against him begins to look watertight . . .

N

R7

I. J. PARNHAM

THE MAN WHO TAMED LONE PINE

Complete and Unabridged

LINFORD
Leicester

First published in Great Britain in 2015 by
Robert Hale Limited
London

First Linford Edition
published 2019
by arrangement with
The Crowood Press
Wiltshire

A catalogue record for this book is available
from the British Library.

ISBN 978–1–4448–4013–1

Published by
F. A. Thorpe (Publishing)
Anstey, Leicestershire

Set by Words & Graphics Ltd.
Anstey, Leicestershire
Printed and bound in Great Britain by
T. J. International Ltd., Padstow, Cornwall

This book is printed on acid-free paper

Prologue

'Orson's late,' Reagan Trask said.

Upton Fletcher shrugged. 'Perhaps he filled Ashton with so much lead he's struggling to drag him back into town.'

Reagan laughed, while Upton's brother Elmore looked outside through the saloon window.

'That's the only way it can end for a man with a death wish,' Elmore said.

Upton nodded, but Elmore continued to look out the window, so Reagan turned in his chair to see what was interesting him.

Beacher McCoy had gathered a group of men outside the stable, who were exchanging opinions with much arm-waving. Their animated behaviour suggested that news had arrived from Snake Town about the showdown between Orson White and Ashton Clarke.

The end of the debate came when

Beacher pointed at the Lucky Star saloon. Then the men headed their way.

Reagan turned from the window and leaned back in his chair to enjoy his whiskey, as did his two colleagues. Reagan assumed Beacher was coming here to give him the news, but he didn't need to hear the details of what had happened at the showdown.

Since a town meeting last week, money had been on offer to whoever tamed Lone Pine by dealing with the gunslingers who had been destroying the town.

Ashton Clarke had stated his intention to collect the money. Yesterday he had issued Orson White with an ultimatum to either leave with his fellow guns, or meet him at noon in the nearby ghost town of Snake Town.

Orson had accepted the challenge and he'd taken six of his guns with him, leaving only Reagan and the Fletcher brothers in Lone Pine.

Either Ashton or Orson would be returning, and Reagan had no doubt which man it would be. So when Beacher came into the saloon he considered him, with a raised whiskey glass in one hand and a smile on his lips.

'I gather you have news,' Reagan said.

'Sure,' Beacher replied.

Beacher glanced at his colleagues standing on either side of him, Lawrence Stacks and Paul Jackson. These three men were the leaders behind the decision to raise money for a town tamer.

Behind them were five other men who had backed the decision with their own money. Reagan couldn't help but note that for the first time they looked at him without fear.

'Who's coming back from Snake Town?' Reagan asked, putting down his whiskey.

'Just the one man,' Beacher said as the delegation spread out. 'And it's not Orson White.'

'But Orson had six men with him!'

'That didn't do him no good when he was facing Ashton Clarke.'

3

Reagan stared at Beacher with openmouthed shock, but the delegation must have agreed their actions beforehand as with decisive speed the seven men moved on. The three leading men drew guns while the others advanced on Reagan's table.

Reagan stood up quickly, but one of the advancing men reached him and shoved him back against the table. Reagan righted himself and threw a punch at his assailant, but the blow didn't land when another man grabbed his arm.

Then, in short order, he was bent over the table and disarmed. While Reagan struggled without effect, scuffling sounded as Upton and Elmore were knocked to the floor and secured. Then Reagan was stood up straight and turned to face Beacher and the others.

'Orson White was the most fearsome shot I've ever seen,' Reagan said, still disbelieving of the tale he'd been told. 'Nobody could have survived a showdown with him.'

Beacher shrugged, then signified that Reagan should be turned to the window. Outside, it was clear that the news must have spread already as the townsfolk were emerging out on to the main drag to look at a lone rider who was approaching the saloon.

With a wince Reagan noted that this man was Ashton Clarke.

Beacher moved forward to stand at Reagan's side.

'Except somehow one man did,' he said.

'Somehow,' Reagan agreed.

1

Five years later . . .

'It's time to stop running and fight,' Reagan Trask said.

Beacher McCoy didn't look as if he could do either. He dropped to his knees and pressed his forehead to the ground.

He dragged gasps of air into his lungs, then forced his head up to consider his pursuer. Reagan was standing with the sun beside his head, ensuring Beacher didn't get even the shade from his shadow.

'We put you away for five years,' Beacher said between gasps. 'You deserved every day you spent in jail, so you didn't need to come back.'

'Except we reckoned we had unfinished business.'

Beacher nodded; the brief respite

appearing to give him strength, he kicked off from the ground.

With his head held low he ploughed into Reagan's legs and drove onwards. His sudden action caught Reagan by surprise and he tumbled forward on to Beacher's back.

Beacher kept moving and with a shrug of his shoulders he fought his way out from under Reagan's sprawling body. Then he regained his feet and broke into a run.

Reagan also got to his feet and laughed, enjoying seeing Beacher showing some fight.

With his head down Beacher ran towards a group of three boulders twenty paces away. His breath came in ragged bursts and he pumped his arms as he tried to gather more speed. He'd halved the distance to the boulders when he stumbled over a stone.

He was keeping his head so low down that he couldn't avoid sprawling all his length. He slid along the dirt for several feet before coming to a jarring halt, then he slapped both hands to the ground.

With his arms shaking he tried to raise himself, but his feet slipped in a patch of loose dirt and he succeeded only in scrambling forward on his hands and knees.

The boulder was only six feet away when the Fletcher brothers Upton and Elmore stepped out from behind it, making him stop.

Reagan paced forward to stand behind Beacher. Without any hope of mercy in his eyes, Beacher raised his head to consider the three men. His gaze rested on the guns they had drawn and aimed down at him.

'I tire of this,' Elmore said.

Upton grunted that he agreed.

Reagan fired. Lead slammed into Beacher's back, making him drop down to lie on his chest.

With a grunt of effort he raised his head, but the brothers had already turned their backs on him, leaving only Reagan looking at him.

Reagan winked. Then he fired again, making Beacher's head slam down into the dirt.

★　★　★

'Have you been to Lone Pine before?' Shackleton Frost asked when he drew his horse to a halt on a rise that looked down on the town.

'Nope,' Nathaniel McBain said. 'I didn't know this place was in our territory.'

'It's on the edge, but Sheriff Ashton Clarke keeps his town under control. So it's been a while since he last had to call on my services.'

Nathaniel nodded. 'In that case, we could face a tough assignment.'

'They're all tough, so we just have to make sure we're tougher.'

Nathaniel gave a supportive snort of laughter as they moved off down the rise.

He and Shackleton had worked together for over a year. Their primary

10

tasks were to escort reluctant men to court and to escort even more reluctant prisoners to Beaver Ridge jail.

Lone Pine had a permanent court and a jailhouse, so, bearing in mind Shackleton's high opinion of Sheriff Clarke's abilities, Nathaniel assumed they would escort a dangerous prisoner. This town was the furthest Nathaniel had travelled from Beaver Ridge, so the possibility of a week-long journey with a potentially difficult prisoner made him pensive.

'What happened the last time you came here?' he asked.

Shackleton glanced at him oddly, as if Nathaniel ought to know the answer, before dismissing the matter with a sigh.

'It was when Ashton Clarke tamed Lone Pine,' Shackleton told Nathaniel, who shrugged. 'Five years ago the town saw a heap of trouble from Orson White and his lowlifes, so they called in a town tamer. Five years on, Lone Pine is a peaceful town and nobody remembers Orson.'

'It sounds like Ashton Clarke is an impressive man.'

'He sure is. Clarke challenged Orson to a showdown in the ghost town of Snake Town so that no innocents would get caught in the crossfire.' Shackleton pointed over his shoulder indicating the direction of Snake Town. 'Orson was a fearsome guntoter and he had six gunslingers with him, while Clarke was alone. Nobody knows how he did it, but Clarke killed them all.'

Nathaniel emitted an approving whistle. 'What was your involvement?'

'After the gunfight, Reagan Trask and two other men who had associated with Orson were still drinking in the Lucky Star saloon. When word of what Clarke had done came in, the townsfolk overcame them and threw them into the jailhouse. They were tried and I was hired to take them to Beaver Ridge jail. That's how I got started in our line of business.'

Nathaniel smiled, enjoying hearing a fact that his partner had never revealed about himself before.

'And Clarke stayed on in Lone Pine as sheriff?'

'He did, and he's made sure the mistakes that happened five years ago, which nearly let Orson destroy that town, don't happen again.'

'Except now he wants your services again.'

Shackleton frowned, acknowledging this was a concern. So they rode on down to the main drag in silence.

When they reached the town Nathaniel watched every person they passed, trying to gather a feeling for the townsfolk's mood. The few people who were outside didn't look at them, which made Shackleton cast Nathaniel a worried look as they dismounted outside the law office.

They went inside, finding only a deputy on duty. He was sitting at a desk facing the door and he regarded them with concern from under a lowered hatbrim.

Even when Shackleton introduced himself and Nathaniel and confirmed their mission, the deputy still rubbed his jaw nervously.

'I'm Deputy Paul Jackson,' he said. 'And I sure am pleased you got here quickly. The trial's tomorrow.'

'You must be sure of a conviction,' Shackleton said with surprise.

Jackson raised his hat to run fingers through his hair, his gaze darting past them to the window to watch someone walk by the law office.

'It's as clear-cut a case as they come, and as I knew it'd take you a while to get here, I thought it best that I moved quickly.'

'If you're expecting trouble the sooner we leave with the prisoner after the trial the better.' Shackleton smiled. 'So you can relax now.'

'I can't even think about relaxing until the trial is over, and then I can't help but think about all the trouble that'll be heading my way.'

'I'm sure Sheriff Clarke will have the situation under control, and that he welcomes having a deputy who takes his duties seriously.'

Jackson gulped. 'I doubt that.'

Shackleton glanced at Nathaniel, who shrugged, acknowledging that Jackson's answers hadn't alleviated his concern about the mission.

'Perhaps we ought to agree the details about this trial with Sheriff Clarke?'

Jackson shook his head. 'That won't do no good. Sheriff Clarke *is* the man on trial.'

2

Upton Fletcher cracked his knuckles while his brother Elmore propped Irvin Atwood up against the wall beside the workshop door. Then Upton moved to kick open the door, but Reagan Trask raised a hand, halting him.

He winked at Upton, then, with an exaggeratedly polite action that made Upton and Elmore chuckle, he rapped on the door. Muttering sounded within before Lawrence Stacks opened the door a fraction.

'I'm afraid you're too late,' Lawrence said, looking around the door at Reagan. 'I'm just about to close up for the evening.'

Reagan smiled, then stepped forward to plant a foot in the door.

'That's no problem,' he said in a calm tone. 'I just want a quick word with you.'

Reagan and the brothers had been released from Beaver Ridge jail the previous month. They had immediately returned to the area, but they hadn't spoken to Lawrence yet and Reagan noted Lawrence's unconcerned expression that suggested he hadn't recognized him yet.

Lawrence glanced down at the foot, clearly weighing up his chances of being able to close the door hard enough to make Reagan withdraw it. He sighed and stood back to hold the door open.

Reagan glanced around the workshop, observing the line of coffins propped up against the wall and another one lying on a workbench, which Lawrence was currently working on. He leaned back and nodded, this encouraged Upton to take one of Irvin's arms. With Elmore's assistance they dragged him into the doorway, making Lawrence gasp with concern.

Irvin was the owner of the Lucky Star saloon and Reagan knew that Lawrence usually called in there for an hour after work. The beating Irvin had received meant he wouldn't be doing that tonight.

Even with Upton and Elmore's help Irvin struggled to walk: he stumbled into the room with his head lowered, causing Lawrence to hurry away to collect a chair, which he placed before the workbench. Upton and Elmore deposited Irvin on the chair, making him groan. He sat hunched over, looking down at the floor.

Blood dripped from his mouth and splashed on the floor between his feet. He raised a hand to wipe his lips, but then with a groan he thought better of making the attempt and let his hand drop down into his lap.

'I'm no doctor,' Lawrence said. 'I can't help him.'

'You might well be the only one who can help him.'

Reagan gestured. Upton moved in and grabbed the back of the injured man's head. Then he drew it back to let Lawrence see Irvin's bruised face.

'What happened to you, Irvin?' Lawrence asked, going down on one knee so that he could share Irvin's eyeline.

Bruises and scrapes covered both cheeks, one eye had shut and blood was oozing from his split lip.

'These men gave me some trouble,' Irvin murmured, then winced as his speaking made a fresh dribble of blood well up in the corner of his mouth. 'I have no idea why.'

Lawrence rummaged in his pocket for a kerchief to stem the bleeding, but then the danger he was in registered and he stopped searching. He looked up at Reagan.

'Why did you do this to him?' he asked, getting to his feet.

Reagan advanced on Lawrence, making him take an involuntary pace backwards that brought him up against his workbench. The coffin shook and rattled.

'Irvin is a respected member of this town,' he said. 'In fact he's so respected that tomorrow he'll serve on the jury at Sheriff Clarke's trial.'

Lawrence gulped. 'Nobody is supposed to know the names of the jury.'

'Except I do, so I know you have good cause to be worried, seeing as how you'll be the foreman of that jury.'

'If you've come here to threaten me you've wasted your time. I won't give in to intimidation and I'll ensure that tomorrow justice is delivered, whether that be in finding Sheriff Clarke guilty, or in finding him innocent.'

'Noble words, but are they backed up with noble actions?'

Reagan gestured, making Lawrence tense, but when Upton and Elmore moved it was towards Irvin. Upton delivered a stinging slap to his cheek that rocked Irvin's head to one side before Elmore slapped his head the other way.

Then Upton drew back his fist, but before he could hit him Irvin fell forward. With no control of his movements, he slid out of the chair and slumped on to the floor.

Upton shrugged and dragged him

back into the chair. Then he rolled his shoulders as he prepared to hit him anyway. 'Wait!' Lawrence cried, halting him. 'If you're going to punish anyone for standing up for justice, punish me.'

Reagan shook his head. 'I don't reckon that'll work. I know your kind. You're a man who enjoys proving he's right, no matter how much pain you have to suffer.'

Lawrence tore his gaze away from Irvin to look more closely at Reagan. His eyes opened wide as, surprised, he clearly worked out who he was. He turned his gaze to the other two men, then groaned.

'I remember you from five years ago,' he said. 'You were associates of Orson White.'

'And I remember you, and I know you care about others, so I reckon you'll want to save Irvin from suffering any more.'

Lawrence gulped, acknowledging that he was right, but he didn't reply immediately, so Irvin got a thump in the stomach and a punch to the jaw that again made him slide to the floor. Once more, he was raised on to the chair.

'All right,' Lawrence said with a weary sigh. 'Stop hurting him and tell me what you want me to do.'

Reagan raised a hand that told Upton and Elmore to back away from the injured man.

'Irvin won't be fit enough to serve on the jury tomorrow, and I reckon one or two others will back out, too.' Reagan laughed, making his colleagues chortle. 'But you'll be there, discharging your duty.'

'I can understand that you men hate Sheriff Clarke, but you have to accept I can't ensure everyone else finds him guilty.'

Reagan laughed. 'You're making a big assumption about what I want from you.'

'I don't know what you mean.'

Reagan walked over to Irvin and raised his head so that Lawrence could see his damaged features. Then he directed a significant glance at Lawrence's current project.

'Then I'll explain,' he said. 'And unless you want to make another coffin, tomorrow you'll do exactly what I tell you to do.'

★   ★   ★

'I'm pleased to see you again, but I'm sorry it's in these circumstances,' Shackleton Frost said.

Sheriff Clarke nodded and rolled off his cot to come to the front of his cell.

'I'm pleased to see you again, too,' he said, 'but I had hoped someone else might come. Escorting me to jail is sure to be tough on you.'

'I've always dealt with my prisoners fairly, no matter who they are. If it comes to that with you, I'll discharge my duty without prejudice.'

'I'm sure you will. I remember that about you from the business I sent your way five years ago.'

For a while the two men stood in

silence, Clarke looking as if he was unwilling to mention the subject that Shackleton obviously wanted to ask him about, and Shackleton finding he didn't want to ask it. But Deputy Jackson had reluctantly agreed to let him talk to the prisoner for only two minutes, so he moved closer to the cell.

'What happened?' he asked in a low tone.

'They say I killed Beacher McCoy in cold blood. He was found shot up in Snake Pass.'

'I won't insult you by asking the obvious question, but why would anyone think such a ridiculous thing?'

Clarke spread his hands. 'I'm the man who tamed Lone Pine. Everyone knows what I'm capable of doing.'

'But back then you did what you had to do and wiped out men who were destroying this town. I haven't been here long, but I can see Lone Pine is a mighty fine town now.'

'It is.' Clarke sighed. 'But if you were hoping to meet a few old friends while

24

you were here, you'll be disappointed. Beacher was one of the few people in Lone Pine who would have remembered the way things used to be back then.'

Rattling sounded behind Shackleton as Jackson put a key to the jailhouse door. Shackleton offered a thin smile.

'That's unfortunate.'

'You're not listening to me.' Clarke raised his hands to grip the bars and pressed his face up between them. 'Hardly anybody is left from those days. They just keep on disappearing.'

3

'How long do you expect this ridiculous excuse for a trial to last?' Shackleton asked when he and Nathaniel reported to the law office in the morning.

Deputy Jackson frowned, his bloodshot eyes and sallow cheeks making him appear even more tired than he had done yesterday.

'Right now I can't even be sure there'll be a trial,' he said.

'I'm pleased someone's finally seen sense. What's happened?'

Jackson opened his mouth to reply, but then he furrowed his brow and leaned back in his chair to look a little longer at his visitors.

'I gathered yesterday that you know Sheriff Clarke. Is that a long friendship?'

'I met Ashton just after he had tamed this town.' Shackleton gestured at

Nathaniel and added, 'But he's never met him.'

Jackson rocked his head from side to side and then nodded.

'That sounds broadly fair to me. I'd be obliged if you'd head over to the court now and see if they'll let you serve on the jury.'

Shackleton took a step back in surprise.

'Why? Haven't they got twelve men already?'

Jackson rubbed his jaw, seemingly already regretting making his request.

'If you're going to serve, I can't answer that.'

'That won't matter none because we can't serve. We don't live here and we work for Beaver Ridge jail. If Clarke is guilty, we'll be the ones who'll take him to jail.'

Shackleton waved an arm as if hinting that these were only a few of the reasons why this was a bad idea. Jackson only shrugged.

'I don't see any conflict there.'

Shackleton shook his head and looked at Nathaniel for support, but Nathaniel smiled.

'I agree with Deputy Jackson,' he said. 'Ever since I started working for you, you've told me that to do our job effectively we have to avoid getting personally involved. As we've always done that, I reckon we can be impartial enough to serve on a jury.'

Shackleton conceded Nathaniel's point by returning his smile. Then he turned back to Jackson.

'We'll head over to the court then.'

As it turned out, Shackleton's misgivings were unfounded. Within moments of offering their help the clerk of the court whisked them away into a room behind the court.

Ten men were already gathered. They were sitting around a table sporting bored expressions that didn't change when Shackleton and Nathaniel came in.

'It seems there'll be a trial, after all,' one man said, then he introduced himself as Lawrence Stacks, the fore-man of the jury.

His low tone suggested he wasn't as pleased with this development as Nathaniel would have expected him to be. The rest of the jurors eyed them with scorn as they sat to join them in waiting.

An hour passed in silence punctuated only by the sounds of industry coming from outside as the preparations for the trial were resumed. When the clerk of the court returned he ushered them into the courtroom.

The court was packed with people eager to watch this case, while the accused looked a haunted man. Shack-leton had spoken warmly of this man and his achievements, but Clarke presented none of the assurance and determination he had expected to see.

Clarke slouched in with his head lowered and even when a few people murmured supportive comments to him he only raised his head briefly, only to lower it again when others grumbled darkly.

Nathaniel had seen enough trials to

pick up on the prevailing mood. The accused was worried, reinforcing Deputy Jackson's opinion that the case was clear cut. Worse, many of the watching people believed Clarke was guilty, while the rest hoped that he wasn't.

Despite his determination to remain impartial, over the next hour Nathaniel found himself being swayed to take a contrary view to the one the trial appeared to be taking.

As he had seen many trials, and during his colourful past he had been on the receiving end of justice, he knew he wasn't being presented with the full truth.

Only two witnesses came forward. From the lively muttering between the lawyers and the judge and their frequent moments of fluster, he gathered that more people should have spoken up, but they weren't here. He also gathered that not all the evidence was available, for undisclosed reasons.

The evidence he did hear sounded believable to Nathaniel.

Deputy Jackson testified that even though he'd known the victim Beacher McCoy for several years, until recently he'd never had to deal with him as Beacher had behaved himself. But recently Beacher had incurred gambling debts and he'd resorted to petty theft.

After several short spells in the jailhouse had failed to make him change his ways, Jackson had wanted to give him a longer time in a cell, but instead Clarke had given Beacher an ultimatum to leave town. Beacher hadn't taken the hint and with hours to go before his deadline he was still lurking around town.

Then he had disappeared, never to be seen alive again, although several days later Jackson had heard that the sheriff had been seen arguing with Beacher. Then Clarke had bundled him into the back of a covered wagon, which three unidentified men had driven off.

Jackson delivered the final piece of his statement in a low tone with his head lowered. His reason for doing this became apparent as the person who had told the deputy about this event wasn't prepared to testify in court or even to have his name mentioned.

The defence lawyer didn't object when the prosecution lawyer poured scorn on the validity of this testimony.

The only other person to speak up was Temple McCoy, Beacher's father, and his arrival at the stand made Nathaniel flinch. He hadn't made a connection from the name before, but he knew Temple.

They had known each other around ten years ago when Nathaniel had worked in Monotony, and he knew Temple to be a decent and honest man, so he listened intently to his testimony.

Temple had heard that Beacher was getting into trouble and he had come to town to help him. But Beacher having left, he'd taken heed of the tale Jackson had been told. After a week of searching for Beacher, he'd ended up in Snake Pass close to the abandoned town where Clarke had gained his reputation by killing Orson White.

At the mid-point in the pass he had found Beacher's body.

This revelation made the audience murmur until the judge quietened them. Nathaniel reckoned it was the location rather than what Temple had found there that concerned everyone.

Beacher had been shot twice and he had clearly been left for dead. But he had survived for long enough to identify his killer. With his dying actions he had used a forefinger to scrawl a name into the dirt around his head.

He had drawn a star followed by the name Ashton Clarke.

When Temple had first arrived in Lone Pine he had talked only with Deputy Jackson, so he'd returned to town with the body to ask him if he knew of someone called Clarke. Jackson had explained that this man was his boss, and Temple's surprise had convinced the deputy that he was telling the truth.

The defence lawyer expressed doubt

about Temple's claim that he didn't know of Clarke or his reputation. Temple rebutted the allegation, and no matter how much the lawyer tried to poke holes in the story, he kept to his tale.

In the end the lawyer offered the opinion that Beacher might have been writing a plea to the law to help him, but he'd died before he'd finished his message. He didn't sound convincing and Temple pointed an angry finger at him, seemingly ready to say more, but the judge silenced him.

Then Sheriff Clarke took the stand. With his head lowered and while using a low tone that ensured the court remained quiet to hear him, he told his tale.

His story was a simple one: that since Beacher had started getting into trouble his deputy had dealt with him. Aside from telling Beacher to leave town, he'd had few dealings with him.

Then Clarke raised his head and reported that at the time, Beacher's disappearance hadn't struck him as odd as he wasn't the first long-time citizen of Lone Pine to leave town unexpectedly recently. His comment silenced the court, but neither lawyer pressed the matter and, with that, the case closed and the jury retired.

'That all seems clear to me,' Lawrence Stacks said as soon as the jury were locked in their room to embark on their deliberations. 'I suggest for the sake of appearances we ask for dinner to be sent in and we deliver our verdict after eating.'

This suggestion gathered a round of nods and approving grunts. Nathaniel hadn't intended to take the lead in the discussions, but everyone's attitude made him speak up in surprise.

'Sheriff Clarke is a lawman who has served this town with distinction,' he said. 'At the very least we owe it to him to give this case serious consideration.'

'We're doing that by giving the case the level of consideration it deserves.'

'But you can't just find him guilty

without talking about it.'

'I'm sure nobody here thinks that. We're finding him innocent.' Lawrence looked around the room, receiving numerous nods. 'Unless anyone thinks there's any validity in the unfounded accusations we've heard here today.'

Everyone spluttered and looked aghast, making it clear that Nathaniel was the only one who had found the evidence interesting. He looked at Shackleton, but his boss didn't meet his eye and instead he sat at the table set in the centre of the room.

Nathaniel sat beside him, but he said nothing more until they had been provided with food, which everyone tucked into eagerly. Then he spoke quietly with Shackleton.

'I gather you didn't find anything odd about the trial?' he said.

Shackleton shot him a narrow-eyed look, then spoke loudly so that everyone could hear him.

'I reckon it's best that whatever anyone has to say, they say it openly to the group,' he said.

At the other end of the table Lawrence nodded.

'All men are equal here and we can all share ideas openly,' he said. 'I've already stated that I heard nothing in the court that made me believe Sheriff Clarke killed Beacher McCoy, and even if he did, I reckon he had good reason. If you have a different opinion, speak up.'

'I reckon you just summed up my misgivings. If the sheriff had good reason, he wouldn't have hidden it and, given this man's recent troublemaking, everyone would have understood. Except he denied having any dealings with him, which is odd.'

'I'm sure that's because he didn't deal with him.'

'Which means Deputy Jackson lied, as did Temple.'

Lawrence shook his head. 'Deputy Jackson only reported on what someone had told him, and the father only reported on what he had seen, which amounts to nothing.'

'It takes courage for a deputy to speak up against his own boss, but maybe you'd think differently if the person who made the claims about the sheriff bundling Beacher into a wagon had spoken up.'

'Maybe I would, but I'm ruling only on what I heard in court, and not on my opinion about rumours we didn't hear.' Lawrence frowned. 'Clearly our clerk of the court didn't brief you well.'

Nathaniel leaned back in his chair and smiled.

'He didn't. Then again, he looked harassed. I gather he struggled to find twelve men who were prepared to sit on the jury in here, just as he struggled to find anyone who would bear witness out there.'

Lawrence's eyes flicked away, that being the first sign that he shared Nathaniel's misgivings. When he looked back, he reached for a sheet of paper.

'This might be a good time to cast the first vote,' he said.

Most of the jurors grunted that they agreed, while those who didn't cast exasperated glances at Nathaniel, as if this process was already trying their patience. Wisely, Nathaniel didn't object and he cast his vote, folded the paper, and placed it before Lawrence.

The voting was carried out with an air of anonymity, but Nathaniel noted that Lawrence read his vote last and that what he'd written made him sigh before sitting back in his chair.

'We have eleven votes cast for not guilty,' Lawrence said. He paused, giving time for most of the jurors to look at Nathaniel. 'We have one vote for not sure, which I blame again on our clerk for not explaining the process properly. We vote either for guilty or for not.'

'I'm aware of that,' Nathaniel said. 'But I don't want anyone to think that I disagree with them. My vote is what I think about what I heard: that I'm just not sure.'

Lawrence nodded. 'So how would

you suggest we proceed?'

'For the sake of Temple McCoy and the memory of his dead son, I reckon we need to talk about this some more.'

Lawrence closed his eyes in irritation while everyone else groaned.

4

'You any calmer now?' Shackleton asked when he brought Nathaniel's third whiskey of the evening to their table in the corner of the Lucky Star saloon.

'Nope,' Nathaniel said. He considered Shackleton and then sighed. 'I guess I'm not used to fighting my battles on my own.'

'You stood up for what you thought was right, which you were entitled to do as a member of the jury. It matters none that nobody agreed with you.'

'Even you.'

Shackleton shrugged. 'I stood up for what I thought was right.'

'You didn't. You never said nothing all afternoon.' Nathaniel took a gulp of his drink, regretting voicing his concern the moment he'd spoken.

'I cast my vote and we found Clarke

innocent,' Shackleton said levelly. 'The matter should end there, except I can see from your furrowed brow that you don't want it to.'

Nathaniel swirled his drink as he chose his next words carefully. He didn't want to have an argument with his friend, especially not after he'd argued with every other man in the jury room all afternoon.

'I just think there was something wrong about that trial and I'd have welcomed knowing that I wasn't the only one to think that.'

'I'd have supported you if I thought you were right.' Shackleton adopted a lecturing tone. 'Every prisoner we escort is innocent and a victim of bad justice, according to them. As I told you when you started working for me, the only way to complete our assignments is not to get personally involved. So we treat everyone fairly, take them to jail, and we let others worry about their guilt.'

'I agree, except today we had to

adjudicate on a man's guilt.'

'We did, and I applied the same rules. I didn't get involved. I listened to the evidence and it amounted to nothing. If we'd found Sheriff Clarke guilty based on a rumour and a message in the dirt, every lawman would face a court based on their prisoners' complaints.'

'In other words, you based your decision on the decency of lawmen like Sheriff Clarke?'

'Sure.'

'That sounds to me like you were getting involved. You trusted that your old friend Clarke would tell the truth, and so you concluded the others were lying.'

Shackleton gave Nathaniel a long look, letting him know he would make the obvious retort before he uttered it.

'And it sounds to me as if you trusted that your old friend Temple McCoy would tell the truth, and so you — '

'Temple wouldn't lie. He's a good man.'

Shackleton pointed a stern finger at Nathaniel, but then dismissed the matter with a shake of the head.

'Get some sleep and get this worked out in your own head. We have a long journey ahead of us tomorrow and I don't want to spend that time arguing about this.'

Nathaniel swirled his drink. 'Neither do I.'

Shackleton nodded. With him not continuing their disagreement, Nathaniel searched for something to say that didn't involve the day's events, but when he failed he got up and headed to the door.

Despite Shackleton's suggestion that he try to put today's events from his mind, he didn't want to move on without speaking with Temple. He figured that even if he couldn't help him, the least he could do was to pass on his condolences.

He didn't know where to start looking for Temple, so he headed to the law office. When he glanced through the window Sheriff Clarke wasn't there, but

Deputy Jackson was talking to the owner of the Lucky Star saloon, Irvin Atwood.

Irvin had been serving drinks when they had arrived yesterday afternoon, but not afterwards, and Nathaniel saw the reason when he noticed the livid bruising on his face. The exchange of words was intense, the deputy gesturing while Irvin stood with his shoulders sagging.

Nathaniel couldn't hear most of what was said, but Temple's name was mentioned several times.

When Irvin shook his head and turned to the door, Nathaniel didn't want to appear as if he'd been snooping, so he moved away from the window. He melted into the shadows and a few moments later Irvin came outside.

As Irvin sloped off, Nathaniel figured that, as a saloon owner, Irvin would hear gossip. He might be able to help him.

At a cautious pace Nathaniel followed Irvin, his interest growing when Irvin didn't head back to his saloon but instead sidled off towards the quiet end of town. Irvin started looking around, as if he was worried that he might be followed.

Nathaniel slowed down and let Irvin get ahead, but he stayed close enough to watch him move through the shadows. When Irvin reached a stable he slipped inside with a neat sideways movement.

His sudden disappearance took Nathaniel by surprise, but he maintained his pace and when he reached the stable he stood by the door while looking inside from the corner of his eye. Enough light was streaming in to let Nathaniel see most of the interior; he couldn't see Irvin so he quickly stood back.

An open door was at the back of the building so, Irvin's actions now appearing strange, Nathaniel hurried inside and went to the door. He couldn't see Irvin, but only one building was close enough for him to have reached it with ease.

Nathaniel moved on to a workshop. It had no windows and a single door, but light was emerging through gaps in the wood.

Nathaniel put an eye to several gaps. He heard Irvin talking with another man, but he couldn't see either of them although he could see a row of coffins propped up against the wall. He couldn't hear the words, but Irvin's tones were low and the other man was angry.

After several terse exchanges, Nathaniel recognized the other voice as belonging to the man he'd been looking for: Temple McCoy. This discovery made him move on towards the door, but before he reached it the door flew open.

Irvin shuffled into the doorway, waving a dismissive hand at Temple.

'I helped you, but this is too much,' Irvin said. He moved to leave, but then stopped when he saw Nathaniel approaching.

Irvin was standing in a stream of light coming from inside and Nathaniel was in the dark, so Irvin narrowed his eyes while edging back through the door. This proved to be an unwise course of action when Temple appeared behind him holding a gun raised high.

Temple rapped the stock down on the back of Irvin's head. Without making a sound Irvin crumpled to his knees, then toppled over to lie on his chest.

Temple hurried forward to stand beside him, concern written on his furrowed brow despite his action, but the moment he saw Nathaniel he turned the gun round in his hand and aimed it up at him.

'Who's there?' he demanded.

'It's me, Nathaniel McBain.'

Temple furrowed his brow, then softened his expression.

'Nathaniel, from Monotony?'

'I'm pleased you remember me.' Nathaniel stepped into the light. 'I thought you'd welcome talking to an old friend right now.'

Temple sighed. 'I assume you heard what happened to my son.'

'I was at the trial today. I didn't think Beacher got the justice he deserved.' Nathaniel waited until Temple lowered his gun a mite. 'But I didn't expect to walk into an argument.'

Temple gestured at Irvin's still body. 'Irvin came to offer the same kind of sentiment. I didn't want it to end this way.'

'I'm sure Irvin didn't either.'

Temple conceded Nathaniel's point by holstering his gun; Nathaniel knelt beside Irvin.

'I don't want to get involved in whatever you argued about, but I'll get Irvin back to the Lucky Star saloon so he can rest up. Then we can talk.'

Temple nodded and so Nathaniel took hold of Irvin's shoulders. Temple made no move to help him, but slowly backed away.

Nathaniel had raised Irvin to a sitting position when a noise sounded near by. He looked around while Temple moved into the doorway.

The noise came again. This time Nathaniel identified the sound as that of someone groaning inside the workshop. Temple put a hand to the door and moved to swing it closed, but when he saw Nathaniel's alert posture he stopped.

'Stay out of this,' he snapped. 'Just do what you said you would and get Irvin back to his saloon.'

'Who's in there?' Nathaniel said. 'What's going on here?'

Temple edged the door from side to side and then slapped it, seemingly making a decision. He swooped down on Nathaniel and in a lithe movement dragged him to his feet.

Nathaniel didn't resist: he let Temple walk him into the building, where he saw the reason for Temple's suspicious behaviour.

On a workbench in the middle of the room a man had been strapped down with his limbs stretched out and secured to the four table legs. When Temple walked him closer to the bench, Nathaniel recognized the captive as Sheriff Clarke.

5

On a table by the wall tools had been strewn about. A stove had been opened and the end of a poker lay inside, although the stove had yet to be lit.

'As you can see, this is the man who killed my son,' Temple said in Nathaniel's ear. 'I'm now getting the justice I should have got today in court.'

Nathaniel shook his head. 'All I'm seeing is an understandably angry man who isn't thinking straight.'

His comment made Clarke look at him, letting Nathaniel see that the sheriff had been badly beaten. Livid bruises and scuff marks marred one side of his face, a gash cut across his forehead and over his nose, and one eye was closed, all of which suggested he'd been hit in the face with a metal bar.

'He's not got the guts for this,' Clarke said. 'He should have just slunk out of town like the low-down snake he is.'

Temple frowned, clearly torn between attacking the sheriff again and working out how he should react to Nathaniel's arrival. As Temple muttered an oath, Nathaniel looked again around the workshop. He saw that Clarke's taunt was probably justified.

The tools looked as if Temple had riffled through them as he tried to work out which one he could use to torture Clarke, while the unlit stove spoke of an intention that Temple had been unable to carry out.

'Listen to the sheriff,' Nathaniel said. 'I remember the man I used to enjoy a drink with and he wasn't the sort of man who could get the truth out of someone in such a barbaric way.'

Temple shook his head. 'Then that's where you're wrong. I reckon I was about to hear everything, but then Irvin arrived.'

'Irvin didn't look pleased with what you were doing either.'

'If Irvin wasn't such a yellow-belly, I

wouldn't have to do this. Irvin was supposed to be on the jury, but he backed out, leaving that bunch of good-for-nothings to provide the verdict they'd been paid to deliver.'

Nathaniel tensed. Temple must have sensed his shock as he turned away and stood over Clarke. Temple had shown no sign that he knew Nathaniel had been a jury member, but Nathaniel decided not to mention this, reckoning that in his fragile state of mind Temple's reaction would be bad.

Instead, he moved around the bench to stand on the opposite side.

'So you're convinced this man is guilty,' he said, adopting a level and soothing tone.

'All the witnesses said so.' Temple waved an angry hand at Clarke. 'Even if they had as much decency as Irvin had and failed to turn up at court.'

'I'd guess from the marks on Irvin's face that he'd been beaten and threatened. The others who didn't come to court probably faced the same problem.'

Temple shot Nathaniel an incredulous look.

'You don't say! When I last met you, you were a deputy sheriff, and I can see you haven't lost your deductive powers.'

Nathaniel smiled, hoping Temple's sarcastic comment meant he was starting to calm down and act like the man he remembered.

'And so you decided to repay one injustice with another by beating Clarke?'

'No. I decided to get to the truth my own way, and before the night is through I'll have it all.'

Nathaniel glanced at the lawman, who peered up at him with contempt, as if he'd not picked up on Nathaniel's attempt to talk Temple round.

'What has he said so far?'

Temple snarled, seemingly unwilling to answer, but Clarke took that decision away from him when he rolled his head to the side to look at Nathaniel.

'If you don't want Shackleton Frost to escort you to jail, free me now,' Clarke said.

Nathaniel edged forward to the bench. 'I'm trying to end this situation without any more unpleasantness.'

He waited until Clarke nodded, but that made Temple roar with anger and turn on his heel. He stormed to the stove and grabbed the poker. Then he came charging back with the poker held aloft ready to work off his anger on Clarke's body.

Clarke cringed away for as far as his bonds would let him, but, Temple's attention being on his captive, Nathaniel slipped his hand to his gun. When Temple reached the bench, he raised the gun into Temple's line of sight.

Temple still moved to dash the poker down across Clarke's chest, but Nathaniel gave him a warning shake of the head, halting him.

'You're siding with the wrong man,' Temple said. 'People say that a whole heap more people than just my son have disappeared after being taken to Snake Pass. I can't let him get away with that.'

'That might have happened, but you

can't harm a man based on a rumour that he's responsible.'

'I'm not.' Temple gestured with the poker at Clarke. 'Look at him. He's done wrong and he knows it.'

While still watching Temple, from the corner of his eye Nathaniel glanced at the sheriff, who now had both eyes closed, and was looking as tired and worried as he had been in the court. Whether that was through guilt or through anger about the situation he found himself in, Nathaniel couldn't tell.

'If you believe you know the truth, then walk away from this,' Nathaniel said. 'I know you. You're not a killer.'

Temple jerked his arm higher, seemingly ready to defy Nathaniel. Then with a muttered oath he swirled around and hurled the poker away with such force that it sliced into the wall and stopped with half of the metal jutting out of the wood.

He cast a sneering glare at Clarke, then with his head down he sloped off towards the door.

'You're right,' he said with a defeated air. 'This is over.'

Nathaniel nodded. 'You're doing the right thing. We'll see what we can do to clear up this mess.'

Temple gave Nathaniel a long look. 'Which is?'

Nathaniel couldn't find an answer. Temple opened the door and took a pace outside. Then, as though startled he looked down. When Nathaniel looked past him he saw that Irvin was no longer lying outside the door.

'At least that means he's all right.'

'That's not the problem,' Temple said. 'He must have gone to fetch help.'

Nathaniel shrugged, pleased that this would help end the situation; he relaxed even more when he saw people moving through the darkness towards the work-shop.

'Don't worry. I'll help you explain what happened here.'

'We won't get the chance.' Temple shot a worried glance at Nathaniel before looking outside again. 'Those men are armed.'

This didn't surprise Nathaniel and he moved to place a reassuring hand on Temple's shoulder, but then he had to step back when a gunshot sliced into the door beside him.

As Temple ran inside, Nathaniel swirled round. Three men were approaching. Their forms were just outlines in the dark, but he could see the guns they brandished.

He raised his hands in a placating gesture, but that made the three men swing their guns round to aim at him. Nathaniel winced and hurriedly followed Temple back into the workshop.

'I'll do the talking,' Nathaniel said, pressing his back to the wall beside the door. 'You free the sheriff.'

Temple stood before the bench with his shoulders hunched, looking defeated, but he shook his head.

'I can't free this man,' he said.

Nathaniel glanced outside and noted that the men were no longer visible. Since they seemed not to be making an immediate move, he figured that the only way to reduce the trouble Temple faced was to help Clarke. He moved away from the door.

'In that case, you talk them round while I free him.'

Temple glared at Clarke, looking as if he was planning to hit him again. However, with an angry slap of a fist against his thigh he moved past Nathaniel to the door. But when he reached the wall he drew his gun and glanced through the doorway, his alert posture that of a man seeking targets.

'The moment they come into sight I'll give them all the talking they can cope with.'

Nathaniel rocked back and forth on his heels, then decided to leave the sheriff bound to the bench. He hurried back across the room to remonstrate with Temple, but a ferocious burst of gunfire sliced through the doorway, forcing him to scurry for safety to the opposite side of the doorway.

'These men sure are determined.'

Temple cast Nathaniel an irritated glance.

'Of course they are. These men have come to help Sheriff Clarke, and that means they're the same men as frightened the witnesses and bought off the jury.'

Nathaniel still hoped that Deputy Jackson might be one of the men outside, but when gunfire again thudded into the door, he didn't argue. He drew his gun, making Temple grunt with approval, and edged closer to the door.

He recalled what he'd seen outside on the way to the workshop, judging that the only places where the men could take cover was beside the stables. They would then have to run across open ground to reach the workshop.

He jerked his head through the door and confirmed that nobody was close by. Then he held his gun out through the doorway and fired a quick shot, aiming high on the stable wall.

'That was a warning shot,' he shouted. 'We want an end to this, so hold your fire.'

Long moments passed in silence, then Temple looked at him and shook his head.

'There's no reasoning with these people,' Temple said. 'They're ruthless men who want to protect their secrets.'

'We don't know that.'

Nathaniel was prepared to say more, but the gunmen made words unnecessary when they started a sustained volley of shots that peppered along the wall and in through the doorway.

Both men inside had no option other than to keep away from the door. In the brief lulls in firing, Nathaniel guessed the men's intent when he heard rapid footfalls approaching to his right.

He caught Temple's eye and signified where he thought the gunman had stopped. Temple wasted no time before edging outside.

Temple blasted a shot along the length of the wall, then jerked back as a returning shot caused splinters to fly from the door above his head. Nathaniel reckoned if he risked edging out again the gunmen would have him in their sights; Temple must have had the same thought, as he kept inside, slipping only his hand outside to fire blindly twice.

Nathaniel followed Temple's example and stayed inside while shooting, although he fired at the stables, this time lowering his aim to just above head height.

Within moments gunfire rattled outside. Temple and Nathaniel stepped backwards a pace. The first two gunshots from outside hammered into the wood of the doorframe, but Nathaniel didn't see where the next two shots landed.

When the gunfire petered out Nathaniel again hurried forward. This time he sprayed gunfire wildly around outside before moving back from the door.

A volley of rapid shots sounded in return. The blasts were so close together it sounded as if a dozen men were firing, not just the three whom Nathaniel had seen.

'They have reinforcements,' Temple said unhappily.

'I'm not so sure,' Nathaniel replied.

'This time most of those shots weren't aimed at us.'

Sure enough, from over to their left Jackson spoke up.

'This is Deputy Jackson,' he called. 'I don't know who's out there and I don't care what this gunfight is about. I've come to help Sheriff Clarke.'

The man standing beside the workshop hissed an urgent question. A few moments later a returning comment made him move along the wall, away from the door.

'It sounds as if the gunmen are retreating,' Nathaniel said, looking at Temple with a smile of relief.

Temple didn't return the smile; he glared across the workshop at the bound sheriff.

'Forgive me if that doesn't give me any cheer,' he murmured.

'It should,' Nathaniel told him. 'You're in trouble, but I'll speak up for you and — '

'I don't want that. If Jackson finds you in here, it'll just complicate matters. You've been a good friend in trying to help me and I appreciate that. Now go and leave me to face the consequences.'

There hadn't been any further gunshots outside for a while. The silence outside gave Nathaniel the impression that the first group of gunmen had gone. He figured that the cautious Jackson would make a move for the workshop before long, so he headed to the doorway.

'If Clarke mentions my involvement,' he said, 'I'll admit what I did here. Otherwise, I'm obliged that you want to protect me.'

'He won't talk,' Temple said.

Nathaniel glanced outside, seeing nothing but darkness, but then he registered Temple's exact words and the dull tone in which he'd spoken. He turned back to find that Temple had raised his gun and was aiming it at Clarke's head.

Nathaniel shouted a warning to Temple and broke into a run. He was several paces away and he doubted he'd be able to reach Temple in time, but thankfully Temple's hand shook with an uncontrollable tremor and he struggled to keep the gun still.

Nathaniel kept running and then leapt forward, caught Temple around the chest and barged him aside. The action made Temple let loose a gunshot that clattered into the wall opposite; then both men went down to the floor, where they slithered along until they fetched up against the wall.

Temple struggled, trying to extricate himself from Nathaniel's grip, but Nathaniel held on to him.

'I know you didn't want to do that,' Nathaniel said.

'The court didn't judge Clarke and you can't judge me,' Temple answered grimly.

Outside, Nathaniel heard scurrying footsteps as Jackson approached.

'I can't, but I reckon that others will.'

6

'I didn't expect to see you again,' Lawrence Stacks said, his wide-open eyes showing that he already regretted opening the workshop door.

Reagan Trask swaggered into Lawrence's workshop with Upton and Elmore flanking him. This time they didn't have an injured man with them.

'We thought we'd come to congratulate you on your performance on the jury,' Reagan said.

Lawrence turned away. He ran a hand along the coffin lid that he had been constructing, then walked round the workbench until he faced Reagan over the coffin.

'I did my duty, which I would have done without your threats. As it turned out, I would have still cast my vote in the same way, which means you hurt Irvin for nothing.'

'It wasn't all for nothing. I proved one thing.' Reagan looked Lawrence up and down, then sneered. 'No matter how much you value doing your duty, you still have a price.'

'You're not the only one who proved something. Your actions showed that you're worried.' Lawrence waited until Reagan snarled, then he leaned forward. 'So state your business and make it quick. I'm a busy man.'

Reagan glared at Lawrence as though preparing to snap back a retort, but then dismissed the matter with a shrug and walked in a circle, a fist opening and closing.

'There's to be another trial shortly because of what happened in this workshop last night. You'll be the foreman of the jury again, and this time you'll make sure the verdict is the right one.'

'I've tried to ignore the details of this case in order to remain impartial, but from what I gather Temple McCoy was found standing on this very spot. Sheriff Clarke was lying on this bench and Temple was holding a smoking gun. Only the quick actions of one man stopped Temple killing the sheriff. If you're planning to threaten me you'll be wasting your time again.'

'I won't.' Reagan stopped his pacing and stood in front of Lawrence. He leaned forward with his hands placed on the edge of the workbench. 'Because you'll ensure that the jury delivers the same verdict as the last time: innocent.'

Lawrence stepped back, unable to hide his surprise. Upton and Elmore laughed.

'That might not be possible,' Lawrence murmured. 'Temple's already confessed to everything.'

Reagan shrugged, then with a roar he swept the coffin off Lawrence's workbench and sent it crashing to the floor. The coffin stood upright for a moment before toppling over, making the sides collapse inwards and the lid to spill into the centre of the debris.

'Then it's your job to make it possible,' he said.

* * *

'Your assistant Nathaniel did well,' Sheriff Clarke said, joining Shackleton at the bar.

Shackleton regarded the bruising on Clarke's face and noted his stooped posture.

'It's a pity you had to get a beating before he could stop Temple,' he replied

'I'd have suffered more if he hadn't stepped in.' Clarke sat on a stool and winced as he rubbed his ribs. 'Then again, I've been on the receiving end of trouble for so long now it might have been a blessing if Nathaniel hadn't stopped him.'

'I don't like hearing you talk like that.'

Clarke shrugged, but everyone in the Lucky Star saloon had now noticed his arrival and several customers crowded around him. His back received numerous slaps of approbation until Clarke complained about the pain and they took to uttering encouraging words.

Clarke received enough offers of free drinks to keep him and Shackleton occupied for the rest of the evening. Clarke accepted the good wishes with grace.

Shackleton was pleased to see this reaction as it confirmed his belief that the trial had been a travesty and he should never have been called here.

When the customers' enthusiastic greetings relented and Clarke was able to enjoy his drink, Shackleton stayed silent, waiting to hear what more Clarke wanted to say about the situation.

'I guess I'm talking like that,' Clarke said, swirling his drink, 'because you're one of the few people who might listen to me.'

'That's showing some faith in me. We haven't talked since you cleaned up Lone Pine.'

'Which means you're doubly qualified. You know what I had to do back then to tame the town, and you haven't seen what's happened since.'

Shackleton sipped his drink while

glancing at Clarke, noting that even without the bruises and the downtrodden expression bought on by his recent experiences, he still looked older and more tired than he'd have expected.

'Are you telling me you haven't enjoyed the attention that being a man with a reputation has brought you?'

'I enjoyed most of the attention. I worked hard for it and I deserved it. We all did.' Clarke flashed a brief smile. 'But as a man with a reputation, not all of the attention has been welcome.'

The two of them stood in silence for a while, letting Shackleton ponder his own theory as to what had happened to Clarke. It was a theory that made him thankful and, for not the first time, surprised that he hadn't suffered in the same way.

Since completing his first assignment in Lone Pine five years ago, by escorting Reagan Trask to jail, he had dealt with numerous other prisoners. Most of them had threatened him or promised to make him pay for doing his job.

So he had always been prepared for someone to come looking for him, but nobody ever had. He could see that things might have been different for a man whose actions had made him an even more obvious target.

'You've survived whatever trouble has come your way,' Shackleton said. 'That should be enough.'

'It should be and at first it was enough. I expected men to ride into town to pick a fight with me just because I was a man with a reputation. When they did I made them regret their arrogance, but before long I tired of it, and then it got worse.'

'You're talking about your fear that other people from those days have gone missing?'

Clarke nodded. 'I have no proof that anything odd has been going on, but over the last few weeks men who have lived here for a long time have suddenly moved on. I didn't worry about it at first, but when it continued happening, I couldn't dismiss it as a coincidence.'

'And Beacher is the first one that you're sure has been killed?'

'His was the first body to turn up.'

'And you reckon you'll be next?'

Clarke didn't reply immediately: he only jutted his jaw, as if wondering whether to explain the full extent of what was troubling him. Then with a nod he appeared to reach a decision.

He filled both their glasses. Then he leaned closer to Shackleton and lowered his voice.

'I could deal with that, as I dealt with all the others who came here to take me on, but I don't reckon that's what's happening. I reckon someone's decided that if they can't kill me, they'll destroy my reputation instead.'

Shackleton gestured around the saloon room, indicating the lively well-wishers who had offered to buy him drinks.

'Look around you. Nobody in here has lost faith in you.'

'Not everyone has, but if you're going to point out the people who were pleased to see me, I could point out the people who didn't come over to congratulate me. Once, you'd have found few in the latter group, but now those outnumber the former.'

Shackleton winced and casually looked around. He hadn't noticed it before, but now that Clarke had mentioned it, even though some men were smiling, more customers were scowling in their direction.

'All because of these unexplained disappearances?'

Clarke sipped his drink while looking straight ahead, seemingly getting his thoughts in order.

'It's not just that. There have been other odd incidents. I'd get congratulated for running someone out of town, even though I'd never seen this person. I'd get told I'd been seen giving someone a beating, but that I'd done the right thing as that person was causing trouble.'

'Again, you'd not beaten anyone?'

Clarke shook his head. 'Nope. I ignored the tales, but the incidents kept happening and they always followed the same pattern. Rumours were reported to me in which I'd done something, and it was usually my using excessive force on a troublemaker.'

'I can guess the rest. When you tried to confirm the rumour you couldn't find the troublemaker, or the person who saw the incident, or even who was spreading the rumour?'

Clarke nodded. 'Nothing tangible happened, until the incident with Beacher McCoy. He *was* causing trouble and for the first time I backed away from dealing with him because I didn't want to encourage the rumours about my heavy-handed methods.'

'It sounds as if Deputy Jackson did the right thing with him.'

'He did, right up until Beacher turned up dead.' Clarke frowned. 'Although that's assuming Beacher was the first one to get killed. Perhaps the other people who are no longer around are dead, too, and their bodies haven't been found yet.'

Shackleton took a long gulp of his whiskey.

'Who do you reckon could be behind this?'

Clarke managed a rare smile. 'I've made a lot of enemies over the years, so I'd have to say that it could be everyone and nobody.'

'At least the trial proved you weren't involved in Beacher's death. That should help your reputation, not ruin it.'

'The trial wasn't convincing, so I doubt it. Evidence was clearly missing, witnesses didn't speak up, and the story was incomplete. It was almost as if the trial had been designed to look suspicious so that even more rumours about me would spread and people would think the opposite to the verdict.'

Shackleton shook his head and thought about what Clarke had said until his silence made him look at him.

'If you're going to figure out who's trying to destroy you, that kind of thinking won't do you no good,'

Shackleton opined.

'Perhaps it won't, but what I can't avoid thinking about is that if I'm right and someone is trying to ruin my reputation, what will they do next?'

7

'He's lasted longer than most,' Reagan Trask said, drawing his horse to a halt now that he could see their quarry ahead.

'I only wish all the others had been as entertaining,' Upton Fletcher replied as he watched Irvin Atwood scurry away.

Elmore grunted with approval and the three men moved their horses on at a steady trot.

As usual, they had released their quarry at sunup at the entrance to Snake Pass. This time Irvin Atwood was the unfortunate victim.

They had selected him because five years ago he had helped to bankroll the hiring of a town tamer. His defiance in bringing Deputy Jackson's attention to Ashton's plight had sealed his fate.

Despite the beating he'd suffered before Ashton's trial, Irvin had shown surprising resilience. They had given him the usual fifteen minutes to run before they went after him, and he had gone to ground amidst a group of boulders that stood close to the entrance.

They had spent most of the morning trying to solve where his trail led, only to find that he'd tricked them. While they had been searching, he had slipped away and then made his way around the side of the pass towards Snake Town, a place where the chase would soon end.

Accordingly, the three men moved into a position where, unobserved, they could see down the main drag. But their caution wasn't needed.

As soon as Irvin reached town, he stomped to a halt. Then he dropped to his knees, his fortitude seemingly deserting him.

He was still kneeling outside the saloon when the three men rode into town. The brothers stayed on their horses while Reagan dismounted and then stalked round Irvin until he stood in his eyeline.

'Why?' Irvin murmured.

'You were there five years ago,' Reagan said. 'You should know why.'

'Getting you locked away for what you did was no reason to hunt anyone down.'

'It was. We want to hear the truth about how Ashton Clarke defeated Orson White.'

Irvin got to his feet and faced Reagan.

'You'll get nothing out of me. I wasn't there and nobody's ever talked to me about what happened out here.'

'Then we'll have to get our fun another way.' Reagan gestured with his gun. 'Now run along and see how far you can get.'

Irvin glared at him with defiance, but when Reagan turned his gun on him he panicked and scurried for the saloon. Reagan watched him flee as he prepared to resume the chase.

But now that Irvin had claimed he knew nothing, he suddenly felt tired of the proceedings. He trained his gun on Irvin and fired.

His shot slammed into Irvin's back, but Irvin still ran on for another two paces before his legs buckled. He fetched up against the hitching rail where he righted himself, then walked around it until he faced Reagan.

He treated Reagan and the others to a defiant snarl. Then he toppled forward to fold over the rail, where he remained with his head and arms dangling.

Reagan watched Irvin until he stilled, then he turned away. He moved on for a pace, stopped and then looked back.

Irvin's posture conjured up an old memory and it gave him a hint of an idea. He rubbed his chin as he allowed the thought to develop before he faced the brothers.

'And now?' Upton asked.

'And now we see how long the next one can survive,' Reagan said.

* * *

'He's your responsibility now,' Deputy Jackson said.

'We'll get him to Beaver Ridge jail safely,' Shackleton said.

Jackson frowned, clearly considering whether he wanted to say anything more, until with a shrug he stood up and faced Shackleton.

'I know that Sheriff Clarke was an old friend of yours and yet you'd still have been prepared to take him to jail. Then Temple tried to kill him and that — '

'I never get personally involved. I just do my duty, like you do, and I treat all my prisoners the same, so escorting Temple will be no different from escorting the sheriff.'

Jackson nodded. He led Shackleton away to the jailhouse, leaving Nathaniel guarding the back door. Nathaniel watched them leave and felt a pang of apprehension.

With time on his hands over the last few days, he had brooded about the situation; even though he'd tried to put it from his mind, Temple's plight still worried him.

Back in the workshop Temple had surrendered to Deputy Jackson without a fight. He'd confessed to everything while confirming that Nathaniel had stopped him from exacting his revenge on Sheriff Clarke.

With the facts being clear, the trial hadn't taken long to organize, so Nathaniel and Shackleton had stayed in town.

He and Shackleton had developed an efficient system for dealing with prisoners, which involved leaving town quickly and by the least travelled and so, hopefully, the least obvious path. As it had been five years since Shackleton had last had to deal with a prisoner in Lone Pine, they had used their time to pick out a route.

Unfortunately, their earlier disagreement about Clarke's trial had ensured that their conversations had been terse. When they weren't carrying out their duties they had avoided each other, so they were both relieved when, earlier today, the trial had started.

What felt like the entire town had crammed into and around the court to hear Temple enter a plea of innocence to the charge of trying to kill the sheriff. His defence rested on his opinion that he was justified in seeking revenge against the man who had killed his son.

The crowded room had given this viewpoint a surprisingly mixed reaction, making Nathaniel pleased that he and Shackleton were planning a quick departure.

Despite the brevity of the proceedings, and the facts not being disputed, the verdict had been a long time coming. The jury clearly had more misgivings about the case than they had had at Sheriff Clarke's trial. After a while the judge had changed his request from wanting a unanimous verdict to accepting a significant majority.

Even then, the tense wait had continued. Nathaniel assumed that someone in the jury was arguing in the same passionate manner that he'd adopted when he had tried to sway everyone's opinion.

It was starting to look as if they would have to wait until the next day for the conclusion, but then the jury had reached a majority decision, which Lawrence Stacks had delivered in an apologetic manner.

Temple was found guilty. He was sentenced to four years.

The deliberations had taken so long that the sun was setting when Nathaniel stood aside to let Shackleton escort Temple out through the back door. This was the first time he and Temple had met since the incident at the workshop, but Temple directed only a wan smile at Nathaniel.

Nathaniel sighed, but for the next hour he put his misgivings from his mind and concentrated on the mission.

They left town at a gallop, heading east towards Beaver Ridge before rounding a hill and then swinging away to the north. Then they embarked on a lengthy circular detour which, they hoped, would confuse any pursuers who would expect them to make for Beaver Ridge by the shortest route.

Ultimately all routes east would take them by Snake Pass, but Shackleton reckoned that by the time they had arrived there, late on the following day, most pursuers would have given up.

They rode on for only an hour after dark, again to confuse any followers who might expect them to travel long into the night, so putting as much distance as they could between them and Lone Pine. They made camp downwind of a large boulder on elevated ground where they could see for miles in most directions.

With little discussion they set about their familiar routine of taking it in turns to sleep while the other man watched their prisoner along with the surrounding terrain.

As it turned out the night passed quietly.

The next day they set off early. They were as quiet as before, other than for a brief conversation in which they agreed that neither man would be likely to face trouble other than from their prisoner.

Even that seemed improbable as Temple had retreated into himself. He rode along with his eyes dead and his posture stiff.

His attitude didn't concern Nathaniel, as he didn't know what he could say to Temple to help him make sense of what had happened. But when they made camp for the second night, having reached one end of Snake Pass on their circuitous route, Temple became more animated.

Nathaniel was still brooding over his own problems, so they had been settled down for an hour before he realized why Temple's attitude had changed. He looked at him over their low fire and offered a smile.

'We intend to skirt around the outskirts of the pass tomorrow,' he said. 'So you don't have to see that place again.'

Shackleton shot him an angry glare, as they never discussed their arrangements with their prisoners, but then with a grudging nod he accepted why Nathaniel had spoken up.

'Obliged for that,' Temple said. 'I have no desire to see again the place where Sheriff Clarke killed my son.'

Other than glancing away Shackleton didn't react, clearly avoiding the potential trap of entering into debate with Temple. Nathaniel limited himself to nodding, but their brief conversation encouraged Temple to talk more.

He uttered only minor comments about the weather and the food, but it was more than he'd managed since they'd left Lone Pine. Shackleton avoided catching Temple's eye and Temple directed most of his comments at Nathaniel, who replied in a laconic manner that didn't invite more general conversation.

When they set off the next morning Temple was still ready to talk a little, but his faltering tone betrayed his nervousness so that even Shackleton spoke to him to assess his state of mind. This appeared to calm Temple as they climbed to the higher ground approaching the entrance to the pass.

Snake Pass was suitably named, consisting of a long winding trail between a narrow entrance and exit. The sides to the pass were difficult to climb, so travellers tended to take the slow but safe route into the pass and then through the abandoned town situated a few hundred yards beyond the entrance.

At a steady rate they surmounted the ridge that stood before the entrance, so they didn't catch sight of whatever was left of the town. Then they rode across higher ground and started working their way back down to ground level beyond the exit.

They had been winding back and forth for an hour down the steep track to ground level with Shackleton leading and Nathaniel bringing up the rear when a distant gunshot rattled ahead of them. The sound made Shackleton hurry on until he reached a flat stretch of ground, where he dismounted and looked down to lower ground.

They had a routine for dealing with

trouble and Shackleton didn't need to give Nathaniel any orders. Nathaniel stopped and ensured that Temple stayed with him until Shackleton beckoned them on.

When they joined him they all moved along to a position where the lie of the land kept them hidden from below.

'Are you sure that was gunfire?' Nathaniel asked after several minutes had passed quietly and with no sign of movement.

'Yeah,' Shackleton said. He pointed beyond the exit to the pass. 'It came from somewhere in Snake Pass.'

Sheer rocks on both sides of the exit from the pass prevented Nathaniel from seeing more than a little of the ground beyond, but when a second shot came he had to agree with Shackleton.

'It sounds as if it's coming from the other side of the exit.'

'Which is good news.' Shackleton waited until Nathaniel raised an eyebrow. 'It means that it's got nothing to do with us.'

Nathaniel murmured that he agreed, but Temple shook his head.

'I hope Sheriff Clarke isn't making someone else suffer in that place,' he said.

Neither of his guards replied, but while each kept one eye on the exit, they resumed their journey down to lower ground. Shackleton directed them to take a route that moved them away from the pass; when they reached flat ground they were a quarter-mile away from the exit.

Nathaniel cast a last look behind them. He saw no movement and they rode away at a steady trot.

The pass was disappearing behind the higher ground they had just traversed when another burst of gunfire sounded. Despite the additional distance they had put between themselves and the exit, the shooting made all three men look around.

This time the shots came in staccato bursts from two sources, giving Nathaniel the impression that the gunfire was being traded, perhaps by men on either side of the pass.

'Even if this has nothing to do with us, I reckon somebody's in trouble,' Nathaniel said.

Shackleton peered at the open plains ahead, across which they could see for several miles.

'It seems like it, but it also looks as if our problems are behind us. We just need to keep riding on to Beaver Ridge now.'

Nathaniel glanced over his shoulder, then gave a reluctant nod. But Temple slapped his bound hands against one of his thighs in a gesture of irritation.

'I can see why my son died when men like you are involved,' he muttered.

Shackleton firmed his jaw and avoided looking at him, so Temple turned to Nathaniel. Temple gave him a long look with a slight narrowing of his eyes, acknowledging their old friendship.

Even without Temple's disapproval Nathaniel hated the thought of leaving while someone else was getting shot up in Snake Pass. He moved his horse on to draw alongside Shackleton.

'You stay with Temple,' he said. 'I'll check out what's happening back there.'

Shackleton rubbed his jaw, then shook his head.

'You won't. We'll both keep moving along with Temple.'

'We can't. Temple was right. We can't just avoid this. Something wrong happened here and it could be happening again. Worse, your friend is caught up in it and the rumours I heard suggest he might even be behind it.'

As Temple murmured under his breath, Shackleton pointed a stern finger at Nathaniel.

'I told you after the trial that you needed to think this through. Clearly you haven't.'

'Except I have, and the more I think about it the more that trial didn't make sense. Even Temple's trial was mighty odd. It took longer than Clarke's did, and Clarke's only lasted for as long as it did because I argued with everyone.'

Temple drew in his breath sharply: he

hadn't been aware of their involvement. Shackleton glanced at Temple and pursed his lips, seemingly to imply that he wasn't being drawn into an argument.

'Now that you've had your say, don't speak of it again,' he said in a neutral tone.

Nathaniel spread his hands. 'If you don't value your friendship with Clarke, there's no point me saying anything more. I just hope I never have to face as much trouble as he's having to cope with, because I sure wouldn't be able to rely on you to help me.'

'If I have a duty to perform when you're facing that danger and if helping you would make it harder for me to discharge my duty, then you wouldn't get my help.'

Shackleton smiled thinly as he spoke, but Nathaniel didn't take the opportunity to lighten his mood and he waved an angry arm at him.

'Hiding behind a determination not to get personally involved would never be a comfort to me.'

'I never said it would. I know that, Sheriff Clarke knows that, and I thought you knew that.'

Shackleton looked ahead, obviously indicating that they should now leave, but, making a sudden decision, Nathaniel turned his horse round. He moved off and headed for the pass at a fast trot.

He expected Shackleton to cut him off or to shout at him to return, but Shackleton didn't respond. For several minutes Nathaniel rode, hunched over his mount's shoulders, but when his rush of blood receded he took stock of the situation into which he was riding.

He had heard no gunfire for several minutes, but he still took a route that veered away from the higher ground so that he could approach the exit of the pass from a different angle. He saw no movement, so when he reached the first sentinel rocks he stopped and dismounted.

He listened; when he heard nothing he moved along sideways, keeping sheer rock at his back. Beyond the high rocks at the exit the pass became wider with large boulders around the side of the pass.

Still moving cautiously he made his way past the high rocks to the first boulder. He slipped behind it. Now that he was in a position where he could look down the pass he waited. After a few minutes someone on the other side of the pass shouted a warning.

A man ran out from between two boulders. He covered only a few paces before skidding to a halt and then, skirting around the side of a boulder, he disappeared from view.

The man was too far away for Nathaniel to recognize him. The same applied to the men who then briefly came into view.

He could tell that they were pursuing the first man. As there were three of them Nathaniel couldn't help but think back to the three men who had ambushed the workshop. Whatever the reason for their activities Nathaniel stepped out from behind the boulder and hurried across the pass with his head down.

A minute after the men had moved out of sight he reached the spot where they had been when he last saw them. A sprawling group of boulders lay ahead, the rocks seemingly having fallen down the side of the pass to lie against each other creating a maze of routes between them.

Nathaniel hurried for the largest gap. He ducked to pass under a leaning slab of rock, then had to step back quickly when slivers of rock burst from the boulder to his side: the gunshot sounding a moment later.

'He must have doubled back,' a man shouted.

'He didn't,' another man called. 'He's over there.'

'I saw a shadow move and heard something.'

'You've been seeing shadows move and hearing things all day. Hold your fire and we'll flush him out.'

Nathaniel reckoned that if his presence had spooked the men, he should continue worrying them, so he edged forward again, ensuring that his shadow would be visible to them.

'He's over there,' the first man called.

Another gunshot rattled, followed by two more, but this time they didn't hit the same boulder as before.

'Got him!' someone shouted with delight, making Nathaniel bunch a fist in irritation.

'You're wrong. The shadow moved again over there.'

Nathaniel heard sounds of the men scurrying across rock fifty feet to his right.

'It might well have done, but that doesn't explain this body.'

A low whistle sounded. 'We really got him this time!'

'So that's another one who didn't last until noon.'

Footfalls sounded. Even though Nathaniel couldn't see what had happened, it was clear that he couldn't help the man who had been hunted down, but he drew his gun as he prepared to get answers.

'I still say I saw something move over there,' one man said.

'If you want to chase a shadow, do it. We're leaving.'

Nathaniel winced and moved back to the other side of the boulder. He clambered on to the leaning slab and lay there on his chest, ready to surprise whoever came looking for him.

Presently he heard grit crunch as someone approached. Then the light level changed as someone moved into the gap.

Nathaniel figured that only one man had come to investigate, so he raised himself slightly as he prepared to jump the man the moment he moved beyond the slab. The man edged forward and his shadow appeared below, but he stopped directly below the slab.

Nathaniel could imagine the man looking around the area beyond the gap. He reckoned that his gaze would surely come to rest on the slab above him. But then, with a grunt, the man turned quickly and the shadow slipped away to the sound of receding footfalls.

Long moments passed in which he

heard no further noises. Then a man laughed, but the sound was some distance away.

He strained his hearing and heard chatter, but it was also faint and he gathered the impression that the gunmen were leaving. Patience was an essential requirement in his job, so when the voices had faded into the distance he continued to wait.

A half-hour passed without him hearing anything more. As the conversations he'd heard gave the impression the gunmen weren't as patient as he was, he clambered down.

He still moved cautiously through the gap and onwards. He looked around and kept close to cover, but he saw nothing until he found the victim of the hunt.

The scene was as he'd envisaged it; the man had been gunned down, his back was holed and bloodied. Nathaniel hunkered down beside the body and turned it over.

He winced. The man was Deputy Jackson.

8

'How much longer are you going to sit there?' Upton Fletcher asked.

'Until I've finished savouring our latest victory,' Reagan Trask replied. He looked at Upton and laughed. 'But do I detect a hint of impatience?'

Upton came into the abandoned law office and walked around the dusty room. It was empty of furniture except for a chair, and a table with broken legs that lay on its side. Reagan could tell he was taking his time in replying so that he could choose his words carefully.

'When we came out of jail I agreed with your plan because you were right that Ashton Clarke had to suffer for what he did to us. But despite everything we've done to him, he's no fool. The longer this goes on, the more time he has to work out who's behind everything. Then he might turn the tables on us.'

'Except I don't reckon he'll work out who's doing this.' Reagan tapped his nose. 'He didn't pay much attention to us five years ago and he's too busy now trying to keep the town from turning against him, which they will do after the latest development.'

Upton smiled and stopped pacing. 'Once word gets out about Deputy Jackson's demise, even more people should doubt him, but I reckon that should be enough. We've been lucky so far that few people have recognized us and we've been able to intimidate the ones who have.'

Reagan frowned and leaned back in his chair to ponder. Over the last few weeks Reagan had found that sitting here in Snake Town at the scene of Clarke's greatest triumph had helped him to think.

Clarke had probably come up with his scheme to defeat Orson White in this room and it was only appropriate that he repay him in kind. Despite that, Upton was right.

They had enjoyed exacting their revenge by destroying Clarke's reputation before they destroyed the man. But their activities would only be a success if the conclusion was the same one that Clarke had delivered to Orson five years ago. Reagan got up and faced Upton.

'Perhaps you're right. Now that we have all the pieces in place to get what we want, maybe we've done enough.'

Upton grinned. 'Elmore will be pleased to hear that. I'll tell him we're moving out.'

Upton turned away, but Reagan raised a hand, halting him. Then he moved across the office to stand beside him in the doorway.

He looked around the office and wondered, as he had often done, what had happened when Orson had stood on this very spot and Clarke had taken him down.

Orson had been blessed with incredibly quick reflexes and an astute mind. Yet Clarke, a man who wasn't a fast-draw gunslinger, had defeated him and then moved on to kill another six formidable gunslingers.

Now everyone remembered Orson as being just another gunned-down outlaw who had too much ambition and too little sense, while the men who had followed him were remembered as a ragtag bunch of good-for-nothings.

Except that that was far from the truth, and one day soon everyone would know what had really happened here five years ago.

Reagan moved on through the doorway and looked down the main drag at Irvin's body.

Like the others they had killed, they had left the body where it had fallen: Irvin was still lying sprawled over the hitching rail with his arms dangling.

The idea that had been on Reagan's mind ever since he'd killed Irvin finally formed itself into a pleasing shape, making him smile. He turned to Upton.

'As we're choosing to end this now,' Reagan said, 'before we go back to Lone Pine, you have one last surprise to prepare for Ashton Clarke.'

'Did you see the men who shot him?' Shackleton asked, his voice gruff, when Nathaniel caught up with him and Temple.

'I only heard them, but I reckon there was three of them,' Nathaniel said. 'I left the body where it was and got out of there quickly.'

'Then you did the right thing.'

Despite his comment, Shackleton's low tone suggested he hadn't forgiven Nathaniel for his defiance, even if it had helped them by ensuring that the incident didn't involve them. Nathaniel could also tell from Temple's lowered head that he'd had the same reaction as Nathaniel on finding out that three men were involved.

Nathaniel turned away from Temple, although he accepted that at some stage on this journey he would have to speak to him privately and find out if he knew anything about these men.

'Doing the right thing would have

been getting there sooner and saving the deputy,' Nathaniel said.

'If you'd got there sooner, I reckon you'd have just suffered the same fate.'

Shackleton glanced at Temple, betraying where his thoughts were leading; Nathaniel reckoned he should make the obvious point.

'Now that a court has found Clarke innocent, it's likely Jackson was investigating what happened to Temple's son and he had the misfortune to come across men who had secrets to protect.'

'It's likely.' Shackleton turned his horse to look back towards the pass. 'So I reckon we have no choice about what we do next. You'll carry on to Beaver Ridge while I collect Jackson's body and take it back to Lone Pine.'

Nathaniel raised an eyebrow in surprise.

'Wouldn't that mean you're doing what you told me not to do and getting involved?'

Shackleton narrowed his eyes. 'Someone has to deal with the lawman's body and you've proved you can't be trusted to do only that. I'll have no problem in letting Sheriff Clarke deal with the rest.'

Nathaniel firmed his jaw to avoid responding angrily to the rebuke.

'Then be careful. The gunmen could have headed back towards town.'

'I'll watch out for them, and don't wait for me. I'll join you when I can.' Shackleton turned away, but then glanced at Nathaniel over his shoulder. 'This is your final warning; whatever happens, we don't get personally involved. Only men who accept that can do our job.'

Shackleton gave Nathaniel a long look, seemingly defying him to retort. When Nathaniel said nothing he rode off at a fast trot towards the pass.

Despite the clear order that left Nathaniel in no doubt that defying Shackleton would lead to him looking for alternative employment, he didn't move on immediately.

He watched Shackleton until he rode out of view. He listened until he was sure Shackleton hadn't encountered any trouble. Then he turned to Temple.

'There'll be just the two of us for a while now, but don't go thinking that'll make things any easier for you.'

'I know that, but I think things will be easier for you.' Temple smiled. 'We can speak openly for the first time.'

Nathaniel conceded Temple's point with a frown. He drew his horse closer.

'Then I'll ask you directly: do you reckon those three men in Snake Pass were the same ones who tried to save Sheriff Clarke back in Lone Pine?'

'I don't know, but it's possible.'

'So does that make you think you tried to kill the wrong man?'

'No!' Temple snapped, his strident answer seemingly being as much for his own benefit as Nathaniel's. 'I reckon Clarke leads those gunmen and they exacted retribution on Jackson for supporting me.'

Nathaniel nodded. 'Deputy Jackson was the only other man who was prepared to speak up, but if someone is taking revenge, that leaves only one other man they might want to go after.'

Nathaniel gave Temple a significant look, but it only made him smile.

'I know,' he said.

Nathaniel moved on and for the next half-hour they rode steadily. The terrain was open, so the chances of a sneak attack were low.

Nathaniel reckoned that the men he'd heard in the pass hadn't ridden this way, but he couldn't be sure. To avoid them, he figured that his most sensible action would be to choose an unexpected route to Beaver Ridge.

He thought back along the route they'd taken to come here, but the only detour he could think of would involve tracking west first. The easiest way to do that would be to double back and head by the pass.

That thought made him smile. The problems he hoped to leave behind all appeared to originate in Snake Pass and he hadn't liked the thought of leaving a mystery unexplained without trying to see what else he could find out.

'I reckon we'll take a different route,' he said. He waited until Temple shrugged, then pointed back over his shoulder. 'We'll head back to Snake Pass and perhaps on the way we might learn something useful about what happened there.'

Temple lowered his head, appearing as reluctant to visit this place as he had been before.

'Won't that violate Shackleton's orders?'

'Perhaps, but that's *my* problem.'

Temple frowned, but he accepted Nathaniel's order without further comment. They turned and moved back the way they had come.

Nathaniel and Temple maintained a slow pace, ensuring that they gave Shackleton enough time to collect Jackson's body and leave the pass. The slow journey made Temple relax; when they reached the exit he was no longer looking pensive.

Nathaniel still rode with Temple at his side so that he could keep one eye on him while looking at either side of the pass. He saw no movement so he veered away to the place where Jackson had been shot up.

They stood over the spot. Nathaniel watched Temple for his reaction, but clearly his thoughts had returned to other matters. He pointed to an area a half-mile ahead.

'That's where I found Beacher,' Temple said.

'That's close enough to where Jackson died for the deaths possibly to be connected, but it's also far enough away for them not necessarily to be connected.' Nathaniel drew closer and offered a sympathetic smile. 'We can track along the other side of the pass if you want.'

Temple shook his head. 'No. I didn't want to come back into the pass, but now that I'm here I ought to go by the place for one last time.'

When they moved on Nathaniel let Temple take the lead. Temple directed them to an area that looked no different from the stark terrain around them. As they had done earlier, they stood over the spot where the body had lain.

Nathaniel could just make out the star that had been scrawled in the ground, although the name itself was no longer visible. Nathaniel backed away to give Temple a few moments alone, and when Temple grunted that he was ready to go they moved on.

They rode quietly along the pass without seeing anything of interest, so when the entrance came into view Nathaniel had to admit he hadn't learnt anything from the detour.

Temple no longer appeared downhearted; he gestured ahead, drawing Nathaniel's attention to the remnants of the town that nestled a few hundred yards from the entrance to the pass. It was easier to ride through the town than to veer away and avoid it, so they directed their horses to ride through the buildings.

Nathaniel peered ahead at the derelict structures that were still standing, but when he saw something unexpected it was closer than the town. A hunched-over form lay on the ground, covered in ragged cloth flapping in the wind, suggesting it could be a body.

Temple and Nathaniel both winced; by the time they reached the form there was no doubt they'd found another body.

'Is this how you found your son?' Nathaniel asked.

'He was just lying there like this one is,' Temple said. 'But I didn't explore this end of the pass, so I don't know if this one died before or after Beacher did.'

Nathaniel dismounted. When he approached the body he could see an arm stretched out from beneath the clothes. Like Beacher, this person had tried to scrawl something in the dirt.

As with Beacher's scrawl the words he'd written were now impossible to make out, although it seemed there had been two words and their length suggested they could have named Ashton Clarke.

'That proves I was right,' Temple shouted from his horse when he saw what Nathaniel had found. 'Sheriff Clarke killed this man, just like he killed my son.'

Nathaniel took his time in replying, hoping the delay would let Temple calm down so that he would reach the same conclusion that he had. He knelt down beside the words scratched out in the ground and pointed at them.

'I agree this message looks exactly like the message that your son apparently wrote before he died.'

Temple opened his mouth to shout a retort, but Nathaniel's matter-of-fact statement appeared to overcome his anger and he glanced away.

'Two bodies, two messages, both probably naming Sheriff Clarke,' Temple said. 'I guess an alternative is unlikely, but it doesn't have to mean what you think it means.'

'I agree there could be plenty of explanations for why it looks as if two people used their last moments of life to scrawl out a message. But I reckon the least likely explanation is that Sheriff Clarke killed them both and that they were both identifying their killer.'

Temple sighed, his downcast eyes seemingly acknowledging for the first time that Nathaniel was right.

'Then what do you reckon happened?'

'You were right that we didn't hear the full truth at Clarke's trial. You reckoned that meant his guilt remained unproven, but perhaps the simpler explanation is that the case against him was fabricated and someone tried to frame him.'

'Which means I tried to kill an innocent man.'

'You did,' Nathaniel said, although he didn't reckon that Temple had asked a question.

'Which leaves the question of who framed Clarke.'

'It does, and as we're near the place where Clarke built his reputation, I'm sure there's a connection to those events.' Nathaniel slapped a leg and stood up. 'But it's not one we need to concern ourselves with. I've learnt enough here and you have an appointment in Beaver Ridge jail.'

'But you came through the pass in the hope that you'd find out what was happening.'

'I did, but the most important question I had to answer was whether it would affect my mission. I reckon that as Clarke is the intended target here, it's unlikely that anyone will come after us, or after Shackleton either. So I'll do what he ordered me to do and not get involved while getting you to jail.'

Nathaniel mounted up and gestured for Temple to ride on towards the town, but Temple didn't move.

'Whether you like it or not, you are involved.'

'When I've dealt with you I'll get involved, but that'll only be to make sure Sheriff Clarke knows about this body. What he does with that information is his concern.'

'That doesn't sound like the man who was so determined to help an old

116

friend that he tried to talk me round to not killing Clarke while fighting off a heap of gunmen.'

'That man was free to make his own decisions. As Shackleton reminded me, this man has a duty to discharge, and the quicker I do that, the quicker I can let the sheriff know about this.'

Temple stared at Nathaniel, and his mouth opened and closed as he appeared to look for a way to talk Nathaniel round until, with a grunt of irritation, he turned his horse away. Nathaniel slipped in behind him and at a steady pace they rode on to Snake Town.

The buildings were largely intact, but there was no sign of life. Nathaniel still cast cautious glances around and when he saw a splash of colour ahead, perhaps from clothing, he drew to a halt.

Temple also stopped. He glanced over his shoulder at Nathaniel, his expression more one of shock than concern. When Nathaniel joined him, he saw the reason for Temple's attitude.

A body lay draped over the hitching

rail outside the saloon.

Worse, that body wasn't the only one here.

9

'This is terrible,' Sheriff Clarke said. Shackleton Frost had led him into the stable so that he could examine the body that he'd draped over the back of his horse.

'I know,' Shackleton said. 'Deputy Jackson seemed a good man.'

Clarke rubbed his face, his eyes were wide and concerned. He glanced at the door nervously as if he expected someone to follow them in and accuse him.

'He was, so what will people say when they hear about this?'

Shackleton drew Clarke away from the body and placed a hand on each of his shoulders to make sure he looked him in the eye.

'I could understand you being depressed after what Temple nearly did to you, but you have to stop feeling sorry for yourself and work out who's behind this,' he told the sheriff.

'That's easy for you to say. You haven't had to put up with watching as everything you've worked to achieve slips away.'

'I wouldn't expect to hear that from the man I knew five years ago. Be that man again and you'll destroy whoever is behind this, but carry on like this and he'll destroy you.'

'I understand what you're saying,' Clarke said with a single nod, but his eyes remained cold.

Shackleton raised his hands, but he doubted that he'd had any effect. He sought an excuse to linger and see if he could find another way to talk Clarke round. He gestured at Jackson's body.

'Do you want help to deal with him?' he asked.

'I don't.' Clarke turned his back on him and stared at the body.

'In that case I'll be in the Lucky Star saloon before I move on out, if you want to ask me anything else.'

'I don't. You've told me everything I

need to know.' Clarke continued to gaze at the bullet-ridden body, so Shackleton headed to the doorway. Then he stopped. 'And thank you for everything you've done, both five years ago and now,' added Clarke.

Clarke's voice cracked on the last words, but he glanced over his shoulder at Shackleton and smiled. On that positive note Shackleton left the stable, but after a few paces he stopped and looked back into the building. Clarke was standing there with a hand resting on Jackson's back and his head bowed.

He looked so defeated that Shackleton couldn't help but think this would be the last time he'd see him alive. He dismissed that thought with a shudder and moved on to the saloon.

In the early afternoon few customers were drinking, but he recognized the undertaker Lawrence Stacks, who was standing at the bar. Shackleton stood beside him and ordered a drink.

'I'd heard you were seen heading back into town,' Lawrence said. 'I thought it must be a mistake.'

Shackleton swirled his whiskey and took a sip.

'I'm just washing the dust away before heading back out.' He glanced at Lawrence, who frowned. Shackleton leaned towards him. 'I guess that means news of why I returned to Lone Pine hasn't spread yet.'

He ordered Lawrence a drink and explained about Deputy Jackson's demise. Lawrence winced.

'I'm getting too much business these days,' Lawrence said when Shackleton had finished. 'I may not have agreed with Jackson about his reports on Sheriff Clarke's activities, but I respected his integrity in stating what he'd been told in open court.'

'As did I.' Shackleton gulped his drink and ordered another one. 'It appears he paid a heavy price for speaking up.'

Lawrence glanced around. Few people were in the saloon and nobody was paying them any attention, but he still lowered his voice.

'Does that mean you're having second thoughts about the way you voted at the trial?'

'No. I knew Clarke from some years back and he was a decent man. I heard nothing at the trial to make me doubt that.'

'So what do you reckon is happening?'

Shackleton knew of Lawrence's reputation as an honest man and he clearly trusted Clarke, but Clarke had confided in him in secret about his recent troubles and he saw no reason to violate that trust.

'It's not my place to worry about that.' Shackleton knocked back his drink and placed the glass on the bar. He looked to the door, then turned back to Lawrence. 'But I'd assume that someone blamed Jackson for testifying in the trial and they took revenge on him.'

'It's possible.' Lawrence sighed. His eyes were troubled, making Shackleton think he wanted to tell him something, but he only shrugged. 'From what I've heard, too many people are questioning Clarke's recent actions. This is sure to make even more people doubt him.'

Shackleton frowned. 'Then hopefully men like you who know the truth will disagree with them.'

Lawrence gulped; this suggestion appeared to concern him more than Shackleton had expected.

'I'll do my best. Clarke needs his friends right now.'

Lawrence glanced at Shackleton's empty glass and, gathering his intent, Shackleton sighed.

'I've spoken with him and I offered him my support, but he knows I have a job to do and that I can't stay.'

Lawrence raised his eyebrows and smiled hopefully.

'Your partner looked to be a good man. I'm sure he'll be fine without you.'

'I trust Nathaniel to complete our mission, or else I wouldn't have left him, but this latest development could mean he'll be facing plenty of trouble now.'

'I don't see how it could. Clarke is at the centre of this, not Temple.'

'Perhaps, but either way, I've always made it my policy to do my duty and not to get personally involved.'

'That must be a great comfort to you.' Lawrence pushed his unfinished drink away. 'Now I have work to do. I hope Jackson's coffin is the last I have to make for a lawman.'

Lawrence looked at him with eyes that betrayed a strong emotion: perhaps guilt or perhaps even shame. As he had done earlier, Shackleton again thought that Lawrence wanted to tell him something, but with a shrug Lawrence appeared to dismiss the matter and he headed to the door.

Shackleton watched Lawrence leave, then at a slow pace he followed him outside.

Lawrence was heading towards the stable. When he got there he glanced inside, but he didn't go in, suggesting to Shackleton that Clarke had moved Jackson's body to his workshop.

Shackleton waited until Lawrence slipped around the side of the stable and then moved off, but he stopped when he saw three men hurry across the stable doorway with their heads down and follow Lawrence round the corner.

Their furtive demeanour gave the impression they had been waiting for Lawrence, and it made Shackleton frown. For a few moments he thought about his earlier speech to Lawrence. Even though he would never admit it to Nathaniel, he had struggled with his commitment to avoid getting involved.

With a sigh he hurried after the three men. He stopped at the corner of the stable and saw them hurry round the far corner, so he moved on.

When he peered round the next corner he saw that the men had waylaid Lawrence. They were all turned away from him, so he couldn't see their faces, but they looked familiar, even if he couldn't place where he'd met them before.

Lawrence was glaring at them in exasperation, making gestures at them to leave, but they ignored these and crowded around him.

Lawrence turned on his heel and barged one man aside. Then he strode into his workshop, slamming the door behind him.

The men faced the closed door until one man turned to the others and shook his head, putting his hands on his hips in a show of anger. His movement let Shackleton see the man's face for the first time; he winced.

Then the other two men moved to enter the workshop, but Shackleton didn't see whether they entered as he jerked back round the corner to ensure they didn't see him. He looked aloft, his mind whirling with the possibilities that this encounter conjured up: he had recognized the leader.

When he heard the door slam he glanced round the corner and saw that the three men had gone inside. Lawrence's attitude had suggested he had met them before, so Shackleton reckoned that even if Lawrence might face some trouble, he wasn't in immediate danger.

He turned away. At a brisk trot he slipped round the stable and hurried to the law office.

When he stepped inside he found that Clarke had returned. He was sitting at his desk staring at the gun he'd placed on the desk; the barrel was pointing at his chest.

He didn't register Shackleton's arrival as he poked the barrel around, making the gun complete a circle and then move on. Only when the barrel was aimed at the door did Clarke turn to him.

From under a furrowed brow he considered Shackleton, who smiled.

'It's time for you to start getting your life back,' Shackleton said. 'Reagan Trask is in town.'

'Who's Reagan Trask?' Clarke asked.

'He's one of the men who associated with Orson White five years ago; however, he lived and I escorted him to

Beaver Ridge jail.'

'There have been so many of them. I no longer remember all their names.' Clarke turned away and resumed poking the barrel around the desk until it pointed at his own chest again. 'What's one more to me?'

Shackleton stared at Clarke in puzzlement, then paced across the office to stand over him. When Clarke didn't react he grabbed his shoulders and dragged him out of his chair.

'You're Sheriff Clarke, and as a lawman it's everything to you.' Shackleton pointed out of the window. 'Reagan followed Lawrence Stacks into his workshop and from the look of it Lawrence has spoken with Reagan before.'

Shackleton shook Clarke's shoulders to emphasize his point, but he didn't need to as Clarke raised a hand, his words having got through to him.

'Lawrence is an old friend. Why didn't he tell me he'd met Reagan?'

'I don't know. Perhaps we should go

and ask him what he knows about Reagan and about Beacher and about all the other things that have gone wrong for you recently.'

Clarke nodded, his eyes brightening for the first time that Shackleton had seen since he'd returned to town.

'Reagan *is* behind this,' the sheriff said, his voice gaining in assurance. 'I remember now. Beacher was one of the men who jumped Reagan and two other gunslingers, Upton and Elmore Fletcher. Then those men took them to Snake Town to identify the bodies before they buried them out there.'

'I didn't know that.'

'After all the problems they'd caused here, nobody wanted them brought back to Lone Pine.'

'Who else was in the group that overcame Reagan?'

'I'm not sure. At the time I was too busy celebrating.' Clarke frowned. 'But Paul Jackson was one of them. I guess that the others were probably the men who have disappeared.'

'So now we know who's behind this and why he's doing it.'

Clarke nodded. Shackleton stood aside to let him take the lead. The sheriff took his gun and headed to the door with Shackleton at his shoulder.

Clarke strode to the stable with purposeful steps, putting Shackleton in mind of the man he'd first met after taming Lone Pine. Clarke maintained his brisk gait as he walked round the stable, only slowing to a cautious pace when he reached the corner from where Shackleton had watched Reagan confront Lawrence.

'Could you gather what Reagan's business with Lawrence was?' Clarke asked.

'They were too far away for me to tell, but Reagan was waiting for Lawrence outside the saloon and he followed him here.' Shackleton said nothing more until they reached the door. 'What's the plan?'

'There isn't one. I'll find out what Reagan wants. Then I'll deal with him.'

'I'm pleased to hear you talking like that again. When I came into the law office, you looked so depressed I was worried you might turn the gun on yourself.'

Clarke glanced at Shackleton, his dead eyes not alleviating Shackleton's concern, but then it was too late for him to worry about it as Clarke shoved open the door and marched in. Shackleton followed him and when Clarke stomped to a halt, he stood at his shoulder.

The situation in the workshop was worse than he'd feared. Upton and Elmore were holding Lawrence against the wall while Reagan held a gun aimed at his chest.

Worse, Reagan was already looking at the door. He smiled when he saw them enter the room.

'I'm pleased you've finally found me, Clarke,' he said casually. 'That means we can now end this.'

10

'That's three bodies now,' Nathaniel said when he came out of the derelict stable.

'Including the one we found out of town?' Temple asked.

'No,' Nathaniel said. Temple winced, gave Temple a sombre look and then moved on to the last building he had to search, the law office.

Temple had been as eager as Nathaniel was to find out what had happened here. He had promised that he wouldn't try to escape, leaving Nathaniel free to explore the town. So far Temple had shown no sign that he would violate that trust and, in a thoughtful frame of mind, Nathaniel slipped into the law office.

Another body lay a few paces in from the doorway.

Nathaniel stepped over it and moved

around the room, fearing the worst, but this was the only body in here. He left the office and joined Temple in the centre of town.

Nathaniel had left the bodies where he'd found them. Now he considered the places in which each of them was lying. The dead men had all been shot, but they didn't appear to have been killed in a single confrontation.

The varying state of each of the bodies suggested they had died over a period of several weeks, but the postures and positions of the bodies hinted at a series of gunfights. As with the first body they had found out of town, the men were unarmed and they wore ragged clothing.

Bearing in mind how he'd heard Deputy Jackson being hunted down he couldn't help but think that these men too had been hunted down and shot.

'In a strange way, seeing this has helped,' Temple said thoughtfully. 'My son wasn't the only victim, so I guess that means he wasn't killed for anything he did wrong.'

'Which leads to the question of what these people *had* done to get themselves shot.'

'I can't help you there.' Temple shot a significant glance at his bound hands. 'After all, I'm only a prisoner.'

Nathaniel managed a smile, then shook his head.

'I know you're as eager as I am to work out what's going on here, but I'm not releasing you.'

Temple frowned, but then edged closer when he realized what Nathaniel's remark implied.

'That sounds to me like you've decided to get involved.'

'I was prepared to postpone reporting on one other dead man out in Snake Pass, but not five. We'll scout around and see what else we can find out. Then we'll head back to town and report to Sheriff Clarke. I reckon even Shackleton will accept that I had to do that.'

'I guess then we have to hope Clarke will do something about it.'

'You've already accepted that the first body proved Clarke didn't kill your son, so don't cast doubt on him again.'

'Except I'm casting doubt on him in a different way. When I found Beacher I hadn't explored this far into the pass, but people had told me I could hole up in the town. Apparently that's what the few travellers who head through the pass usually do.'

Nathaniel frowned. 'It is hard to believe that none of them happened to come through the town or that none of them reported what they'd seen.'

'The only possible answer is that they did tell Sheriff Clarke, and he did nothing about it.'

Nathaniel shook his head, unwilling to accept this possibility, but seeing no other explanation. In a thoughtful mood he moved away to the law office and stood in the doorway.

Then something occurred to him that he hadn't considered before and he called Temple over. When Temple arrived he stood aside to let him see the body.

'From what I've been told, five years ago Orson White was killed here when Clarke tamed Lone Pine,' Nathaniel said. He moved over to stand beside the prone body.

'I've not heard of Orson,' Temple said. 'But then I wasn't in town for long. Who was he?'

Shackleton had talked about Orson when they were riding into Lone Pine and later he'd told him more details. At the time Nathaniel had been worrying about the trial and he hadn't paid much attention, but he remembered two facts.

'Orson got shot up in this abandoned law office and Clarke left his body here. Later, Clarke killed another gunman and left his body dangling over the hitching rail outside the saloon. Presumably it was a warning to the rest, but they didn't heed it as he still shot up another five men.'

Temple cast him a puzzled look; Nathaniel knelt beside the body to see what else he could learn.

'So a body was left dangling just like

the body outside,' Temple said. He shook his head. 'That can only be a bizarre coincidence.'

'Perhaps it is, because I can't think of any reason why they should be killed in a way that resembled a gunfight that took place here five years ago.'

Temple frowned. 'I can't either, but perhaps we ought to check out the other bodies and see if there's anything else to connect them to Clarke's gun battle.'

Nathaniel nodded, then he suddenly realized that even if he hadn't worked out whether his theory was right, they faced a more important problem.

'Wait. It was mentioned at the trial that over the last few weeks other men have disappeared from town.'

'And that's who these men are.' Temple bunched a fist. 'They're all men who lived in Lone Pine, just like Beacher did.'

'And just like with Beacher, nobody appeared to know about it until someone stumbled across their bodies.'

Nathaniel raised a hand when Temple started to repeat his earlier explanation. 'I don't reckon that's because Clarke was told and he didn't act on the information. I reckon it's because anyone who followed the clues and came here to investigate got killed.'

Temple rocked his head from side to side, then with a wince he acknowledged the probable truth of this theory.

'Which means the people who killed them watch the town and wait for someone to arrive,' he surmised.

'And we don't want to end up like . . . ' Nathaniel trailed off, but Temple gave a knowing nod.

'Despite the danger we're probably facing, I'm still pleased to find another clue as to why Beacher was killed.' Temple smiled thinly.

The two men hurried out of the law office. Nathaniel looked up and down the main drag, but he could see no sign that anyone else was in town, so they headed to their horses.

They mounted up and rode off in a

calm manner to give the impression to anyone who might be watching that they were unconcerned. They pursued the path they had been following before they came across the bodies, but they stopped when they reached the edge of town and were facing the end of the pass.

Nathaniel saw nothing ahead to concern him, but Temple murmured with alarm. He drew Nathaniel back.

'We've got company,' he said.

★ ★ ★

'I agree with you,' Clarke said, glaring at Reagan. 'This is where it ends.'

Shackleton backed up these words by stepping forward to stand with Clarke. Reagan glanced at Upton and Elmore, who emphasized the danger Lawrence was in by drawing him forward and then slamming him back against the wall.

'For you it will end, but not for your reputation,' Reagan said. 'That's still got a long way to fall.'

'I'd gathered that this was all about ruining me, even if I didn't know who was turning everyone against me.'

Reagan snorted a laugh. 'I'd figured you weren't the lawman everyone said you were. A decent sheriff would have found me before I found you.'

Clarke shook his head. 'I didn't work out that you were behind this because you were too insignificant for me to remember you.'

'We trusted Orson White,' Reagan snapped. 'You took him on when we were elsewhere, or else you'd never have taken him and the rest down.'

Upton and Elmore grunted in support. Clarke glanced at them and sneered.

'Orson didn't put up much of a fight,' Clarke said. 'One bullet did for him and then I took down the rest of his worthless bunch. If you three hadn't been skulking in the saloon like the no-good scum you are, you'd have got what the others got.'

'We've spent the last five years

wondering if you're right, and when we got out of jail it'd have been easy to test that theory. Except we wanted to make you suffer.' Reagan looked him over. 'I reckon we did.'

Clarke glanced at Lawrence and then at the men holding him, clearly summing up his chances if he were to go for his gun. Reagan's resolute stance and his firm grip on his gun suggested he wouldn't be able to save Lawrence.

Clarke backed away a pace, lowering his head in apparent surrender.

'It did, I'll give you that, but whoever walks out of here will get to tell their side of the story.' Clarke raised his head to face Reagan. 'That man will be me, and what you've done will soon be forgotten.'

Reagan licked his lips, seemingly pleased with Clarke's retort.

'Not this time, because I've arranged one final surprise for you, and no matter who walks out of here, you'll still be destroyed.' Reagan glanced at the door. 'So do we end this here, or do you want to enjoy my surprise first?'

Clarke flicked his gaze around the room, as did Shackleton. Then, with a short bow, Clarke conceded that Reagan had the upper hand.

'I'll see this through.'

Reagan nodded. 'In that case, you'll leave first.'

Clarke turned and made for the door, but he didn't catch Shackleton's eye. Shackleton assumed that the sheriff had yet to come up with a plan, so he decided to wait for the first opportunity to act. He waited until Upton and Elmore had dragged Lawrence away from the wall, then he followed Clarke outside with Reagan walking at his heels.

Shackleton kept alert as he also looked for an opportunity to turn the tables on Reagan. He expected the first chance might come when Reagan disarmed them, but to his irritation Reagan took no risks. He ordered them to throw their guns to the ground and then move aside.

When Upton and Elmore had collected the discarded weapons, Reagan frisked Shackleton and Clarke before directing them to go to the open wagon that stood beside Lawrence's workshop.

A coffin lay in the back; Reagan eyed it with a smirk on his face, an obvious hint that he reckoned he would use it later.

Following Reagan's directions, Shackleton and Clarke got on the wagon and sat to one side of the coffin; Reagan and Lawrence sat facing them on the other side. Reagan pressed his gun into Lawrence's ribs and adopted a relaxed pose that would let him keep the gun still for hours. Upton and Elmore climbed up on to the driver's seat.

Elmore took the reins. Upton sat sideways so he could hold a gun on Clarke. Then, without asking for further instructions, Elmore trundled the wagon away from town.

He took the most direct route, avoiding the main drag, and when they'd moved beyond the last building and the open plains were ahead, he swung the wagon to the right. Shackleton wasn't surprised to find their direction was towards Snake Pass.

Earlier Shackleton had taken a cautious path to reach Lone Pine, but the wagon took a direct route that would reach the pass before sundown. That provided plenty of time for them to retaliate, but Clarke looked around him and not at the men in the wagon, ensuring that if the unexpected were to happen he would not be slow to respond.

As they rode along Shackleton came to accept that Clarke probably didn't want to try anything until they reached their destination and he had found out what Reagan planned for him.

They made good time and when they reached the entrance to Snake Pass the low sun cast long shadows across the route ahead. They veered to the side to trundle past the spot where Shackleton had found Jackson's body, then they continued onwards.

After covering a short distance further Elmore drew the wagon to a halt. Clarke glanced at the ground and then around him as he gathered his bearings.

'Beacher McCoy's body was found here,' he said.

'It was and he's not the only one to die here,' Reagan said.

Clarke said nothing. Shackleton pointed back along the pass.

'I assume you're talking about Deputy Jackson,' he said.

'I'm not,' Reagan replied and gestured at Elmore, who moved the wagon on.

Shackleton glanced at Clarke who was now sitting tensely, as if he'd understood the taunt. Presently Snake Town appeared ahead.

A few hundred yards before the first building, Elmore drew the wagon to a halt.

When Shackleton looked over the side he winced. Another body lay on the ground.

'This behaviour is twisted,' Clarke

said, staring at the body. 'This isn't revenge.'

'I never said this was about revenge,' Reagan said. 'I want answers, and you're the man who'll provide them.'

11

When they reached town Elmore drew the wagon to a halt outside the derelict law office. Reagan glared at Clarke, as if he expected a response, but Clarke stared straight ahead, making Reagan take the lead.

With a snort of derision Reagan gestured at Upton and Elmore, who got down off the wagon and stood in defensive positions around the back of it. Then Reagan indicated to Lawrence that he should get off too.

When Lawrence had jumped down and the other two men were standing guard over him, Reagan signalled to Clarke and Shackleton. Clarke took his time in responding, but Shackleton edged along the wagon and clambered down.

As the three captives were lined up, Clarke continued to present the air of a man who was ignoring proceedings. He looked at a spot a few yards on from him, which happened to be the back of the wagon.

Shackleton presumed Clarke was actually sizing up the situation, so he adopted the same unconcerned air while taking every opportunity to look around from the corners of his eyes. When he saw what was waiting for them, he revised his assumption about the reason for Clarke's behaviour.

Faced with this situation, he doubted that anyone could maintain their composure, so he now presumed Clarke really was depressed and that he had withdrawn into himself. Reagan must have noticed Shackleton's surprise as he came to stand in front of him.

'I see you've noticed what we've done, but have you gathered its significance?'

Reagan gestured as he spoke, inviting Shackleton to turn away from the wagon and look down the main drag. Shackleton did as requested and cast his gaze down one side of town and then back along the other.

'Over the last few weeks people have disappeared from Lone Pine,' he said. 'This is what happened to them.'

'That's part of the story.' Reagan laughed. 'The uninteresting part.'

Shackleton glanced at Clarke, but he kept his back turned and Shackleton couldn't tell if this revelation had shocked him. Lawrence did turn round; he looked at each of the bodies in turn, his expression growing more and more horrified.

When Lawrence finished his contemplation of the scene in front of the saloon, Shackleton looked that way too. The sight of the body dangling over the hitching rail outside the saloon tapped at his memory.

When he noticed a body just beyond the doorway in the law office, he winced. Then he looked at Reagan, who winked on seeing that Shackleton had figured things out.

'You've put bodies into the same places as they were in after the gunfight with Orson White here five years ago,' Shackleton said with a sorry shake of the head.

'It's more than that. On the day Ashton Clarke tamed Lone Pine he killed seven men. Two men died outside the saloon, another in the stable, and Orson White got gunned down in the law office. Then Ashton headed out of town. He killed another man just out of town, a second halfway along the pass, and another near the far exit.'

Shackleton looked shocked. 'That's where you left all the bodies, including Beacher McCoy's and Deputy Jackson's. So you killed people for no reason other than to recreate the appearance of a fatal gunfight.'

'We killed the men who jumped us in the saloon after Clarke's gunfight gave them the courage to act.'

'So the message beside Beacher's body wasn't *about* Clarke, but was a message *to* Clarke.'

'We tried to get his attention, but he just wasn't listening.'

'And now that you've exacted your revenge, Reagan, what next?' Shackleton snapped.

Reagan curled his upper lip in a show of contempt, although his eyes remained lively.

'I'm pleased you don't yet understand why we did this, Shackleton. It proves you didn't know the truth when you took me along with Upton and Elmore to jail, and it proves the truth has remained hidden and that I was right: this was the only way to reveal it.'

Reagan moved round Shackleton, who turned to watch him as he paced to a halt beside Clarke. Long moments passed in silence before Clarke turned his head to look at Reagan, his slow movement seemingly reinforcing the fact that he had yet to look around town.

'What truth?' Clarke asked, his voice low and barely audible.

Reagan smiled. 'The truth about what happened here when you killed Orson White.'

'As Shackleton said: why did you have to kill seven men to get to that truth?'

'Because now we're going to walk around town and visit the bodies one by one. You're going to explain how a no-account man like you took each one down.'

Clarke glanced at the coffin on the back of the wagon.

'Then you'll kill me, I presume?'

'I hope not. If I get the truth, we'll all head back to Lone Pine and you'll tell everyone the real story about the show-down in Snake Town. If you won't do that, you'll get to return in the coffin.'

Clarke shrugged. 'If you kill me, you'll never get to the truth.'

'I won't, but I'll make sure everyone hears my version of events, and bearing in mind how bad your reputation in Lone Pine is right now, it'll be believed.'

Clarke settled his stance and looked Reagan up and down. He frowned, then with an apparently resigned air he turned on the spot to look around the town for the first time.

He gazed at the saloon and the stable, then looked out of town. He finished his perusal of the scene facing the law office.

Clarke shifted his eyes from side to side as if working out how accurate Reagan's recreation of the apparent gunfight was. He nodded.

'Where do you want me to begin?' he asked.

'Start at the beginning and show me how you defeated Orson White, the finest shot I've ever known.'

'I could do that, but the gunfight didn't start with Orson's demise.'

Reagan raised an eyebrow in surprise. 'In that case, just start at the beginning.'

★   ★   ★

'What are they doing?' Temple asked when his patience finally ran out.

Nathaniel waved at Temple to be quiet and moved away from the corner of the building to stand with his back to the wall beside Temple.

'I can't figure it out,' Nathaniel whispered. 'They're just standing there talking and I can't hear most of what they're saying.'

'And you don't recognize the men holding Clarke and the others?'

'No, but there's three of them, and they raised their voices briefly. The leader is Reagan and the other two men are Upton and Elmore.'

'The names mean nothing to me, but these must be the same three men who are behind everything that's been happening here.'

Nathaniel nodded, and made a calming gesture, urging Temple to be silent and not risk alerting the newcomers to their presence. He was confident that so far they hadn't been noticed.

They had seen the men arriving while they were still close to the building and the shadows cast by the low sun ought to have masked their forms. Since then they had stayed hidden.

Nathaniel edged to the corner to look again down the main drag. He found that there had been developments. Upton and Elmore were standing guard over Shackleton and Lawrence while Clarke and the presumed leader Reagan were walking towards the stable.

Clarke was walking slowly while Reagan stayed a few cautious yards away from him, both men presumably fearing deception on the part of the other. Shackleton was watching them, so, accepting that his boss would react if an opportunity to fight back presented itself, Nathaniel pondered on how he might give him that chance.

The nearest building to the wagon was the law office, and he judged that the door was about ten paces away from Shackleton. The surrounding buildings were intact enough to provide cover, so he reckoned he could reach the back of the law office without being seen.

He glanced at Temple. 'Can I trust you?'

Temple raised his bound hands. 'If you want to try something, I won't escape.'

Nathaniel nodded, but Temple kept his

hands raised, shaking them for emphasis until Nathaniel got his meaning.

'I can't release you.'

'Your boss is the prisoner now, and he'll stay that way unless we can help him.'

Nathaniel glanced round the corner of the building and saw that Clarke was standing in the stable doorway. He was gesturing to Reagan with an obvious invitation to enter the building.

A body was inside, and if that was what they were looking at Nathaniel figured they would then visit the saloon and the law office, and the latter was perhaps his better place for mounting an attack. Taking a sudden decision, he hurried away from the corner and started work on Temple's bonds.

'Don't make me regret this,' he said.

'I won't, but I'll make sure the men who killed Beacher do.'

This sentiment made Nathaniel put aside his misgivings and after checking the scene on the main drag he moved on to the far corner of the building.

Temple dallied to see the situation for himself, then followed him.

They walked cautiously to avoid making any noise as they skirted around the back of two buildings before reaching the law office. Nathaniel stopped in a position where he could see some of the town.

He checked the building and confirmed that it had no windows at the back or back exit. He accepted that he couldn't spring a surprise on Reagan, but nobody was visible on the main drag.

Seeing no other choice, he walked at a slow pace, sideways, with his back to the wall until he reached the corner. He peered round it and to his relief everyone was in the same positions as they had been in when he had last looked.

Shackleton and Lawrence were watching the stable on the opposite side of the main drag with Upton and Elmore flanking them. These men were watching their prisoners and they weren't paying attention to Reagan. Inside the stable Reagan and Clarke were a few paces from the doorway and they had their backs to him.

Nathaniel was five paces away from the door to the law office; he contemplated making a move for it, but then Clarke turned round; Reagan turned a moment later.

Reagan's attention was on Clarke, but Nathaniel still jerked back and pressed himself to the wall. He conveyed with a grimace to Temple that he had been lucky not to be seen.

They had to remain flattened to the wall as the two men moved away from the stable. Nathaniel judged their progress by watching their long shadows as they crossed the main drag.

When the shadows disappeared from view he reckoned that they were heading for the saloon.

'We wait until Reagan goes into the law office,' he whispered to Temple.

Temple nodded. 'You take on Reagan. I'll deal with the other two.'

'I'm armed, but you won't stand a chance.'

'That doesn't worry me. I can cause a distraction that I'm sure your boss can use.'

Nathaniel had never lost a prisoner and he hated the thought of doing so now, but in this case he accepted that he had to give his charge freedom to risk his life. He patted Temple's arm and smiled.

'Wait until I give the word. Then don't hesitate — move quickly.'

Temple nodded. He looked straight ahead, taking deep breaths as he rehearsed in his mind how he would make his move. Nathaniel did the same, although he would have to react to any situation that might develop,

Several minutes passed in silence. Then a flicker in the light level alerted Nathaniel a moment before two long shadows appeared close to the wall. The shadows advanced, then footfalls sounded until with a stomping of feet they stopped. Nathaniel heard voices.

'Now tell me about Orson,' Reagan said.

'He died here,' Clarke said. 'What more can I say?'

'This time I expect a lot more than that.'

'I've told you everything I can remember. I was too busy taking care of these people to worry about every detail.'

'Except I'd expect you to remember more details than you have so far. Everything you've told me is something anyone could deduce from where the bodies are lying. Now tell me something I don't know, and start by telling me if the body is in the right place.'

'You were brought out here after the gunfight to identify the bodies. You saw the scene.'

'I did, but I want to know if *you* can remember the scene. So far you've not convinced me.'

Clarke didn't reply. Shuffling sounded while one of the shadows moved out of sight. Nathaniel assumed that Clarke had gone inside; he willed Reagan to follow him.

He looked at Temple to make sure he

was ready to act, but Temple was frowning.

'What did that mean?' he mouthed.

Nathaniel was more concerned with choosing the right moment to act, so he shrugged, but then Temple grimaced and looked past him. Nathaniel turned his head and saw shadows moving quickly.

He risked looking out on to the main drag, then he too grimaced.

He wasn't the only one who had been choosing his moment to act, but to his surprise the other man wasn't Shackleton.

Lawrence was pounding across the dirt and heading for the law office.

12

'Stop right there!' Reagan shouted, but Lawrence kept running.

He had halved the distance to the law office when Shackleton used the distraction to turn on the nearer of his captors, Elmore. Nathaniel came out from his hiding-place at a run with his head down and his gun held low.

Reagan was only three paces ahead, which was closer than Nathaniel had expected. Worse, the low sun was shining into Nathaniel's eyes.

Reagan had raised his gun to aim at Lawrence's chest, but with alarming speed he snapped his head round to look at Nathaniel.

In desperation Nathaniel threw himself to one side. He moved for a half-pace, then his shoulder collided with the wall, sending him back on his original path.

Using a contemptuous backward flick of his arm, Reagan cuffed Nathaniel about the side of the head, knocking him to his knees. A second blow on the back of the head sent him sprawling on his chest.

A gunshot sounded, making Nathaniel wince, but the shot hadn't been directed at him and when he raised his head it was to see Lawrence fold over, then stagger on while clutching his chest. Nathaniel tried to raise himself, but a thudding pain in his head made him feel nauseous and he flopped back down again.

With his cheek pressed to the dirt he struggled to move or even just focus his eyes, but he could only make out the blurred image of Lawrence as he moved closer. Then he must have blacked out, as the next thing he knew Reagan was dragging his gun out of his hand; he could no longer see Lawrence.

Reagan put hands to his shoulders and pulled him to his feet. Then he held him around the chest from behind with one arm while jabbing a gun into his back.

Nathaniel stood with his head lowered; he found the thought of blacking out again comforting but, taking several deep breaths, he made the pain in his head recede and he stopped feeling disoriented. He looked up and winced.

Lawrence's unexpected action had failed before it had achieved anything other than to ruin their attempt to fight back.

On the other side of the main drag Shackleton was lying on his back, feeling the side of his head. Upton was holding a gun on him.

Temple hadn't even managed to get halfway to the wagon before Elmore had turned a gun on him. He was holding his hands high while kicking at the ground in frustration.

Worse of all, Lawrence was standing hunched over and clutching his bloodied chest. Clarke had gone to his aid and was supporting him.

'I need to help him,' Clarke said.

'You won't,' Reagan said. 'All you'll do is give answers.'

Clarke glared at Reagan, but when Reagan raised his gun arm he slipped a hand under Lawrence's chest and supported him. Lawrence stumbled to one side. Clarke tightened his grip and tried to right him, but Lawrence moved another short pace, this time towards the law office.

When Clarke murmured comforting words, Lawrence ignored him and staggered on towards the office. Clarke glanced defiantly at Reagan.

'He's not listening to me. I can't stop him.'

'Just do it or I'll put another bullet in him.'

Lawrence edged forward again. In a sudden move Clarke swung round to put himself between Lawrence and Reagan.

'Nobody else will die because of me,' Clarke said as he helped Lawrence move on.

Reagan tensed, but he didn't fire,

confirming that he wanted Clarke alive — for now. Taking another two short paces Clarke edged Lawrence past the body in the doorway; then they disappeared from view.

Nathaniel figured that even if Lawrence had ruined their chances of fighting back, now that Clarke was out of sight the sheriff might try something. So he stood up straight as he gathered his senses.

'Don't try anything while he's in there,' Reagan muttered in Nathaniel's ear; then he raised his voice. 'Clarke, put Lawrence down on the floor and get back outside.'

Silence greeted his demand. Reagan turned Nathaniel round to face the door while gesturing at Upton and Elmore, who advanced on their captives. Upton dragged Shackleton to his feet and swung him round to face the door. Elmore grabbed Temple's arm and shoved him to the side for several paces, then swung him round.

With Nathaniel on one side of the door, Temple on the other side, and

Shackleton facing it, they waited. Still Clarke didn't emerge. Reagan snarled with irritation.

'You have five seconds to come out,' he shouted. 'Then I start killing everyone out here, one by one.'

Nathaniel relaxed; he was preparing himself to try to tear himself away from Reagan's grasp when Clarke tried whatever he had been planning inside. Several rapid heartbeats later Clarke still hadn't responded to Reagan's ultimatum. Reagan glanced at Elmore, presumably to give him an order.

Reagan flinched when he saw that Elmore was shifting from foot to foot in uncertainty while staring at the doorway.

'I can see Clarke and he's got a gun,' Elmore said when he noticed that Reagan was looking at him.

'He can't have,' Reagan said. 'There was nothing in the law office and we frisked him.'

Elmore raised an eyebrow and looked at the doorway again. Reagan still grunted in disbelief, but then Clarke spoke up.

'You searched me and Shackleton,' he said with a snort of laughter, 'but you never considered that Lawrence would have a concealed weapon.'

'It'll help you as much as it helped him. I have three guns out here and they're all waiting for you to show yourself,' came the reply.

'We both know you won't shoot me. You've gone to a lot of trouble to set up this situation because you want answers.'

'I *do* want answers, but there's plenty of ways I can get them. We were doing this in a way that would have avoided further bloodshed, and we can still do that. The choice is yours.'

'You killed seven men because they jumped you in the saloon, so I don't believe your promises.' The light level beyond the doorway changed as Clarke moved position. 'But you can believe mine. Let those people go and then we'll talk.'

'So we have a stand-off, and that can

have only one result.'

Clarke laughed, the sound easy and confident.

'You sound like Orson did, just before I wiped out him and his worthless bunch, and you'll never find out how I defeated him.' Clarke chuckled. 'Until, that is, you're breathing your last after I've shown you what I'm capable of doing.'

Reagan looked at Elmore, who shook his head. Then he glanced at Upton, who would be out of Clarke's line of sight.

Upton pointed at a spot beside the doorway and gestured, indicating he could sneak up on the law office and then burst in the through the door.

Reagan nodded. Upton released Shackleton and then slipped sideways away from him while directing a warning shake of his head at him. Reagan shifted his weight so that he could cover Shackleton, too, while Shackleton limited himself to glaring at Reagan.

Nathaniel had worked with Shackleton for long enough to interpret his intentions; he watched him carefully as Upton made his cautious way to the law office.

'All right, you win,' Reagan said, speaking slowly while tightening his grip around Nathaniel's shoulders as a warning not to alert Clarke. 'You're right that we want answers and that this is just between the two of us. We'll release our prisoners one at a time.'

'You're doing the right thing,' Clarke said. 'Release Temple first.'

Upton was still ten paces away from the corner of the law office, from where he'd have to sneak along the wall, so Reagan directed a glance at him to hurry him up. Then he took his time in replying.

'I'll release him last.'

Temple tensed and firmed his jaw, seemingly preparing to shout a warning. He must have conveyed his feelings as the shadow of Clarke's leg appeared briefly in the doorway before moving away.

'I should have known I couldn't trust

you,' Clarke said, his tone sounding more disappointed than angry. 'Now you'll never get any answers.'

All three gunmen tensed and faced the doorway. Nathaniel settled his weight on his toes as he prepared to jerk aside and distract Reagan.

Then a gunshot tore out in the law office.

A thud sounded as of someone falling over, making Reagan direct a puzzled look at Elmore, who returned an equally puzzled look; then his expression turned to one of shock. A moment later Clarke's outstretched hand appeared through the doorway; it was only a foot off the ground.

Clarke bunched a fist. Then the hand opened and slapped to the ground.

Long moments passed with no further movement.

'He shot himself,' Elmore said, breaking the silence.

'Why would he do that?' Reagan muttered. He pushed Nathaniel forward.

'To deny us what we wanted, I guess.'

When Nathaniel saw the scene inside the office, he realized that Elmore had been right. Clarke lay on his side with his shirt front soaked in blood and the gun lying in a sticky patch beside his chest.

Reagan shoved Nathaniel aside; with an angry grunt he kicked Clarke so that his lifeless body rolled over on to his front and fetched up against the other body. Then he picked up Clarke's gun and whirled round to glare at his prisoners.

'Don't go thinking Clarke's sacrifice will save you,' he said. 'He's just condemned you all.'

13

To Reagan's orders, Upton moved back to Shackleton pushed him forward while Elmore moved Temple on.

'This is a disaster,' Elmore said when everyone had grouped up with the gunmen. They were now standing in a circle, their captives standing in the middle.

'We destroyed Clarke,' Reagan said, his flush of anger gone as he regained control. 'In fact we ruined him so much he took the easy way out.'

'Except this was never just about taking Clarke down one piece at a time. I've always said we should have done this another way.'

'No other way would have worked.'

'And neither did this one.'

Reagan snarled. He gestured at the stable.

'We aren't finished yet. Take them

over there and we'll talk this through.'

Obediently Upton and Elmore busied themselves with shepherding their prisoners across the main drag to the stable. Reagan stayed behind, glaring at Clarke's body; then with a shake of his head he followed them.

Inside the stable the three prisoners were placed in the far corner. Their captors moved away to the doorway. Upton and Elmore removed the body that had been placed here; then, keeping their eyes watchful, they debated in low tones what they should do next.

Nathaniel tried to listen to what they said, but when he failed to overhear anything he glanced at his companions. Temple was watching their captors intently. Shackleton turned to him and narrowed his eyes.

'What are you doing here?' he asked quietly.

'We were trying to save you,' Nathaniel said.

'That's not what I meant. By now you should be well on your way to

Beaver Ridge. As it is, you're further away than when I left you.'

'Seeing as how you're in a heap of trouble, it's a good job for you that I am here.'

Shackleton glanced at their captors before making the obvious retort.

'Which means you violated my order not to get involved.'

'It's not as simple as that and, either way, *you*'re here, and the only explanation I can think of is that you ignored your own rule.'

Shackleton flared his eyes and didn't reply immediately, seemingly giving credence to Nathaniel's taunt, but their conversation had been loud enough to attract Reagan's attention. He paced halfway across the stable and stopped in front of them.

'We've made Clarke suffer and what we did to him was so bad he ended it all. Now it's your turn to suffer.'

Reagan licked his lips, prolonging the moment before he acted, but to Nathaniel's surprise Reagan then backed away. He continued walking backwards with a smile on his lips until he rejoined the other two, but the smile soon died out when the three of them resumed their tense debate.

'So what do we do now?' Nathaniel whispered from the corner of his mouth.

'We wait,' Shackleton said. He sighed. 'Then we both get involved.'

Nathaniel nodded and even Temple managed a slight tilt of his head. Then they sat back against the wall.

The sun set and the evening dragged on without Reagan making his intentions known. Instead, his group exchanged views in terse utterances that made it clear they weren't happy about Clarke's demise, even though they had set out to destroy him.

Earlier in the evening the conversation suggested they wanted answers about the events of five years ago, but Nathaniel couldn't see why it should concern them as much as it apparently did. A few hours after sundown, and seemingly without coming to any decision, the three captors settled down to rest in the opposite corner.

Presently Elmore and then Upton started snoring; Reagan however sat upright against the wall in a patch of moonlight and watched them.

Without discussing tactics Shackleton and Nathaniel settled down on the ground in positions where they could watch him while also catching a few moments' sleep. As they were used to guarding prisoners, they could keep vigilant while still resting.

The rectangle of moonlight had shifted away from their captors when Reagan woke Upton, who took over the duty of watching them. This process continued at regular intervals throughout the night without any hitches.

By the time the moonlight had given way to the glow of first light, Nathaniel had given up hoping that one of their captors would make a mistake.

Elmore was the last one to guard them. He grumbled to himself about the chill slipping in through the doorway and set about finding a warmer place to sit. He found a spot several yards away from the other two; this position must have been a good one as he soon slipped down to lie on his side.

When he drew his hat down over his eyes to avoid the gradually growing light, Nathaniel nudged Shackleton in the side. With a nod, Shackleton poked Temple, who came alert quickly.

Moving quietly all three men shifted positions, as if they were just moving in their sleep. Finding that that didn't make Elmore react, they sat up. Elmore still didn't move, so, glancing at each other, they got to their feet.

They stood crouched over with postures that would make it obvious they were planning to sneak away, but when even that didn't provoke a reaction they quietly moved towards the doorway. They walked close to the wall in the darker part of the stable, placing their feet to the ground slowly.

With every step Nathaniel expected

Elmore to raise his gun and order them back to the corner after allowing them to hope purely so that he could disappoint them, but they reached the doorway without him showing any reaction. They slipped outside from where they cast last glances at the sleeping men, then they moved along the stable wall.

They reached the next building, then speeded up. They figured that trying to ride out of town would make too much noise, so with frequent glances over their shoulders they hurried on towards the edge of town.

When they faced open ground they stopped to catch their breath. The glow on the eastern horizon had spread to almost directly overhead suggesting sunup would soon come and so their escape was unlikely to go unnoticed for long.

'I went along the length of the pass and I saw nowhere to hide,' Nathaniel said. 'So I reckon we should head to the entrance and try to find somewhere to hole up beyond it.'

'I'm pleased you spent the time when you should have been making for Beaver Ridge to check out the area,' Shackleton said.

Nathaniel ignored the sarcasm; then since Shackleton said nothing else, he moved on towards the entrance at a fast trot. Shackleton slipped in behind him while Temple brought up the rear.

Temple took every opportunity to look back and he was soon lagging behind, but Nathaniel kept going, figuring they could rest and plan their next actions when they reached the entrance to the pass. After running for five minutes he judged they would leave the pass in another five minutes, but when he next looked back Shackleton was also slowing down while looking back to town.

'Come on,' Nathaniel urged. When they both ignored him, with a sigh of frustration he turned on his heel and hurried back. 'Stop wasting time worrying about them coming after us.'

Temple acknowledged his plea by

turning round, but it was to look at Shackleton, who nodded. Then Shackleton turned and both men waited for Nathaniel to join them.

'We've both had the same idea,' Temple said. 'We reckon that our escape was too easy.'

'We had to wait all night to take our chance, so it wasn't that easy.'

'So three ruthless gunslingers who secretly killed the men who captured them five years ago, and who ground Clarke down piece by piece, just happened to fall asleep?'

Nathaniel frowned and kicked at the ground.

'Maybe that escape was too easy, but why let us go?' Even as he asked the question the answer came to Nathaniel. He looked up at the lightening sky and sighed. 'Jackson got hunted down and killed, and it's probable the others were hunted down, too.'

'These people don't just want revenge,' Temple said. 'They want to recreate what Clarke did to Orson and his men while extracting every last drop of pleasure out of it that they can get.'

'I accept that, but that's no reason to give up. We can still reach the end of the pass before they come for us.'

'We haven't given up,' Shackleton said, looking around. 'But now that we know what their plan is, we can turn the tables on them.'

'How?'

'By doing the one thing they won't expect us to do.' Shackleton pointed back towards town. 'We don't try to escape.'

Nathaniel contemplated the harsh terrain ahead, which offered few obvious places to hole up. He didn't welcome the thought of being hunted in the way he'd heard them track down Jackson.

He nodded and they headed back to town. This time they sprinted as fast as they could, the three of them running in a line.

They ran along a path from which the stable was hidden, and in a short time they approached the outskirts of town. As Reagan hadn't appeared yet they slowed, to avoid any chance of their rapid approach being heard, and to get their breath.

When they reached the first building they slipped around the back. Temple dropped to his knees and gasped in air, but Nathaniel and Shackleton looked around as they searched for a way to fight back against Reagan.

As Nathaniel had briefly explored the town he knew that the nearest building was a store. He pointed out a door at the side of the building and beckoned to the others to follow him inside.

He had no significant hope that they would find anything in the store that they could use as weapons. Sure enough, the interior was in as bad a state as he remembered it.

The building had been gutted and even the only interior wall had been demolished, but a window afforded them a good view of the stable, which was two buildings down on the opposite side of the main drag. While Temple mooched around the room and rooted about through piles of mouldering wood for anything they might use as a weapon, Shackleton and Nathaniel walked to the front.

Shackleton watched the stable through the door and Nathaniel peered out of the window at the other buildings.

'I can't remember any of the buildings being in a better state than this one is in,' Nathaniel said. 'So I doubt we'll find anything we can use against him.'

'That doesn't matter,' Shackleton said. 'Reagan has the firepower, so our only advantage is the element of surprise.'

'He'll soon figure out we haven't run. Then he'll return and search the buildings systematically.'

'You're right, so we need to spring a surprise on him before he figures out what we've done.'

Nathaniel smiled, enjoying, after all their arguments, discussing tactics with Shackleton.

'Perhaps we should split up.'

Shackleton was about to nod, then he checked himself and drew Nathaniel away from the window.

'It's too late,' he said.

Both men pressed their backs to the wall between the door and the window as people bustled out from the stable. Temple slipped into the shadows in the far corner of the room, then they awaited developments.

Reagan gave Upton and Elmore orders, his calm tone leaving little doubt that the watchers had indeed been allowed to escape. Even with his back to the wall Nathaniel could see some of the main drag, and Reagan was walking away from the store.

Nathaniel was craning his neck as he tried to work out where they had gone. Then footfalls approached, suggesting that Upton and Elmore were coming their way.

Nathaniel risked moving his head to the side for a fraction, and saw that they were heading across the main drag. They were chatting amiably, seeming to be unaware of where their quarries were. He attracted the attention of Shackleton, who with a brief nod and a wink acknowledged that they would let them pass and then jump them.

'You reckon this will work?' Elmore was asking as they came closer.

'No,' Upton said. 'They don't know nothing. We need to get this over with and find someone who does know.'

'Sure, and now that Reagan's got what he wanted out of this, he should start working with us more.'

'Are you sure? Clarke killed himself before he explained anything.'

The footfalls sounded directly outside the door and Shackleton tensed as he prepared to slip outside the moment the men had passed by.

'I reckon he explained enough,' Elmore said. 'Reagan will figure out the rest.'

Shackleton glanced at Nathaniel and nodded, but the conversation they'd overheard had intrigued Nathaniel and he shook his head. Shackleton shot him an alarmed look that said they had to make their move *now*. Making a sudden decision Nathaniel slapped a hand on Shackleton's shoulder and gripped it tightly.

Shackleton shook his shoulder, but he couldn't dislodge Nathaniel's grip. He stopped, accepting that he couldn't free himself quietly. Then, with an exasperated sigh, he glanced at the door, to point out that Upton and Elmore had now moved past the store and the moment had been lost.

'Why?' Shackleton whispered urgently.

'You heard them,' Nathaniel said. 'They want something more than just revenge.'

'They do, but how does that help us?'

'Because if we can figure out what they want, we might find a way out of this.'

14

Nathaniel glanced outside and noted that Upton and Elmore had stopped fifty yards beyond the edge of town. Upton was looking at the ground for tracks while Elmore was looking further afield. Reagan wasn't visible.

He reported the scene to the others, then set his hands on his hips.

'I agree that these people have different aims,' Shackleton said. 'If you'd let me jump them I'd have been sure to ask them what they're after.'

'It's too late to argue about that now,' Nathaniel said. 'We've all heard and overheard different things, so now we just have to work out what they want.'

Shackleton looked sceptical. He edged closer to the door to look out for Upton and Elmore. Temple came over to him, nodding.

'Reagan is obsessed with finding out

189

how Clarke defeated Orson White,' Temple said. 'He reckons Clarke wasn't as formidable as Orson was. So he set the stage in this town to show the aftermath of the gun-fight, to force Clarke to explain how he'd done it, but I don't reckon the other two care about that.'

'Agreed,' Nathaniel said. 'But to uncover that truth he didn't need to place the bodies in the positions in which they died five years ago.'

Temple frowned. He moved to the window to look around the town. He pointed at the law office, where Clarke's body still lay.

'I got the impression that the only explanation Reagan would accept is that Clarke didn't kill Orson. Perhaps Reagan staged the scene to find out if Clarke had actually witnessed the event.'

Shackleton had been standing hunched over, looking aggrieved as he paid more attention to the scene outside than their debate, but this comment made him avert his gaze from the doorway.

'That's nonsense,' he snapped. 'Clarke

defeated Orson and the other gunslingers.'

'But nobody but Clarke knows how he did it,' Temple said. 'He can't tell anyone now, but maybe he killed himself to avoid people figuring out that he took credit for something he didn't do.'

'The day will never come when I believe the word of a prisoner, and especially one who tried to kill Clarke.'

'I've accepted I did wrong there. Clarke didn't kill my son, but it's likely he didn't kill Orson either.'

Shackleton waved an angry hand at Temple, seemingly lost for words. He looked to Nathaniel for support, but Nathaniel shook his head.

'I reckon Temple is talking sense,' he said. 'If Clarke could take on that many gunslingers, he'd have taken down Reagan without breaking sweat.'

Shackleton shook his head. 'That's not what happened. We shouldn't be questioning Clarke's actions. We should think about Reagan. How come he wasn't here with Orson, but was in the

Lucky Star saloon a half-day away?'

'That's a good point. So what do you think happened?'

'I don't know, and I don't care because the one thing I know for sure is that Ashton Clarke gunned down Orson White and tamed Lone Pine.'

Shackleton's voice rose on the last few words and in the empty room his statement echoed, making all three men tense and then stand still. By means of glances only, they debated whether they had been arguing loudly enough to alert anyone who might be near by.

With a series of nods they agreed that they probably had and that they should move on quickly. Then a creak sounded outside.

A moment later Upton and Elmore burst in through the doorway.

Shackleton was the nearest to the door and Upton delivered a stinging backwards swipe with his gun that caught Shackleton underneath his right ear. It pole-axed him in an instant.

Nathaniel was only a pace further away

from the door; even before Shackleton had hit the floor Elmore tried the same manoeuvre, but, given a moment longer to act, Nathaniel thrust up an arm and jerked his head away.

Elmore's arm slammed against Nathaniel's wrist, diverting a blow that whistled past his chin. While Nathaniel was still off balance Elmore followed through with a forward swipe of the gun; this time it crunched into his cheek.

Elmore hadn't been able to get much force behind the blow but it still made Nathaniel double over. Elmore continued his onslaught with a shove to Nathaniel's side and then a punch to the ribs that made Nathaniel stagger backwards until he crashed into the wall.

Nathaniel steadied himself against the wall and moved to leap back at Elmore, but his opponent slammed a pile-driving punch into his stomach. The blow blasted all the air out of Nathaniel's lungs and he dropped to his knees, gasping and trying to avoid retching.

When he looked up Elmore was

standing confidently before him with his gun raised. Upton was standing over Shackleton, who was shaking his head as he struggled to regain his senses. Upton moved his attention to Temple and then recoiled in surprise when with a great roar of defiance Temple charged across the room.

Upton backed away, raising his gun, his reticence in firing it confirming that their orders were to capture the escaped men alive. Temple seized this advantage by thrusting his head down and leaping at Upton. He caught him round the chest and both men went down.

Elmore moved to one side to hold a gun on them: his caution being justified when Temple planted a firm hand on Upton's gun and tried to wrestle it from his grip. Upton resisted and the two men fought for supremacy.

Nathaniel raised his right knee and settled his weight on his foot while pressing a hand back against the wall. He took deep breaths and then kicked off from the floor.

At the last moment Elmore tore his gaze away from the battling men and advanced on him, so Nathaniel was still rising up when he slammed into Elmore's chest. Elmore dug in a heel and Nathaniel failed to move him, so he wrapped his arms around Elmore's chest and twisted.

Elmore again resisted Nathaniel's attempt to knock him over.

Nathaniel twisted the other way. This time Elmore stumbled to one side and, feeling heartened, Nathaniel twisted even harder.

For a moment the two men stood doubled over until they both went down. As they fell, Elmore's foot slipped from under him and both men toppled over with greater force than Nathaniel had anticipated.

They skidded across the dusty floor before fetching up against the wall, beneath the window. As both men lay on their sides, crunched up, Nathaniel grabbed for Elmore's gun. His hand closed on air.

A gunshot tore out, the sound echoing in the unfurnished room. Then came a groan; it took Nathaniel a moment to register that it had come from Temple.

Heavy thuds sounded, then Upton came into view with his gun held on them. While still struggling Nathaniel looked past Elmore.

Temple was now lying on his side facing away from him, blood spreading from beneath him.

'He knew nothing, and I doubt you do either,' Upton said. 'So I've got no qualms about blasting you away, too.'

Nathaniel tried one last lunge for Elmore's gun. When he failed to find it he nodded in a show of surrender.

Elmore extricated himself from Nathaniel's grasp and stood up. The two gunmen backed away for several paces, each man holding a gun on one of their captives.

Upton gestured at the door. The chance to fight back gone, Nathaniel got to his feet. He moved over to Shackleton, who had now opened his eyes.

Nathaniel tapped a foot against Shackleton's side, making him murmur.

Then Shackleton saw Temple's body. Wincing, he appeared to regather some of his senses.

Nathaniel leaned down and helped Shackleton to his feet. Shackleton rose to a stooped posture, so Nathaniel supported him with an arm around his chest. Then they moved on to the door.

Outside Reagan was pacing along the opposite side of the main drag and surveying the scene with caution. When he saw them emerge he stopped outside the law office and stood with his legs planted wide apart.

Upton and Elmore followed them out. They kept several paces away and made no move to hurry them on, so Nathaniel walked slowly to give Shackleton time to recover.

When they reached the middle of the street Shackleton was walking with greater ease, and by the time they were twenty paces from Reagan he drew himself away and walked alone.

He moved on for several faltering steps until Reagan beckoned them to stop. Upton and Elmore moved on to stand to their sides and facing them.

'You were the worst quarries we've had,' Reagan said. He raised his gun to sight upon Nathaniel, while Upton and Elmore aimed at Shackleton. 'Some people didn't survive until noon, but you didn't even last until sunup.'

'So you enjoy hunting men,' Nathaniel said, raising his chin in defiance.

'Five years ago Sheriff Clarke gave everyone an ultimatum to leave by noon or he'd come looking for them. We're just doing the same.'

'Why should you care? You weren't even here when Clarke killed Orson White.'

Reagan firmed his gun arm to aim the gun at Nathaniel's head.

'You don't know what happened here.'

'And neither do you, or else you wouldn't have set up this situation.' Nathaniel smiled. 'Perhaps now is the time we should discuss what's worrying you.'

Reagan narrowed his eyes, and when

Nathaniel met his gaze he lowered his gun a mite. With an irritated grunt Upton took a step forward.

'Get this over with,' Upton said. 'It's time to move on.'

Reagan raised his free hand. 'We can wait for a few more moments. It sounds to me as if these men might know more than they've let on.'

'They don't know nothing! He's just stalling.'

'He might be, but Shackleton first came here in the immediate aftermath and he might have heard things, while the other two spent time with Sheriff Clarke.' Reagan stared at Upton until he gave a reluctant nod, then he turned back to Nathaniel. 'Tell me what's on your mind.'

Nathaniel took a deep breath and settled his stance, trying to appear confident and not look like a man who was doing what Upton thought he was doing. Quickly he ran through in his mind everything he'd learnt since he'd come here, along with the explanations

Shackleton and Temple had deduced.

'You want to know how Clarke killed Orson White and six gunslingers on his own,' he said, giving himself time to think by stating facts.

'That much is obvious. Tell me something we don't know.'

'The answer, you suspect, is that he didn't, which means he had help, and you're trying to figure out who Clarke was protecting.'

'Again that's obvious. You're trying my patience.'

'He's broken mine,' Upton snapped, while Elmore muttered a supportive oath. 'He's just playing for time.'

'So, are you?' Reagan asked.

Having stated the obvious facts Nathaniel couldn't think where they led him. He glanced at Shackleton for help, but Shackleton was rubbing his forehead as if he was still disoriented, while from the corner of his eye he watched Upton and Elmore, looking for an opportunity to fight back.

Nathaniel looked further afield for

inspiration, considering the bodies they'd positioned around town, hoping he might deduce how this gunfight had played out in reality. He couldn't think of anything that might engage Reagan's interest, and with his hopes of reconstructing the gunfight receding he ended his survey of the town by looking at the law office.

Something about the scene there struck him as odd, but, with Reagan glaring at him and making it clear that his next statement would decide his fate, it took him long moments before he worked out what was wrong.

Then he saw it.

Sheriff Clarke's body was no longer lying in the doorway.

He thought back: he had seen the body this morning when he'd looked around town. He doubted that anyone would have had the opportunity or inclination to move it since then, so the only explanation was the one he wouldn't have thought possible before.

He continued to look around to

avoid anyone else noticing what he'd just seen. Then he faced Reagan. He smiled, his confident expression making Reagan lower his head slightly in interest.

'I'm not bluffing. I know what happened here and you people have provided the answer.' He pointed at each gunman in turn. 'One of you wants to know how Clarke did it and the other two want something else. That's just the way it was five years ago.'

Reagan nodded. 'Go on.'

'Clarke didn't tame Lone Pine out of the goodness of his heart. He was paid to do it, yet he showed no sign of being wealthy. So what happened to the money?'

'You tell us,' Upton shouted before Reagan could answer, confirming that Nathaniel's assumption was correct.

'Five years ago Clarke did deals. The gunslingers would have been willing to turn on each other if the price was right, so he turned one faction against the other and then picked off whoever survived. You figured that might happen and so you stayed in Lone Pine.'

Reagan nodded. 'Orson White was a formidable man. No man would have taken him on.'

'Which means you suspect Orson was really the man who tamed Lone Pine. He turned on everyone and wiped out the gunslingers for the money that was on offer. But then Clarke killed Orson.'

'That's a mighty big assumption, but it's a good one.' Reagan glanced at his gun. 'So how did Clarke do it? And what happened to the money?'

'The answer to the second question follows on from the first.' Nathaniel smiled. 'I reckon Clarke hid in the law office until Orson had killed everyone else. Then he used the money to lure him in there and took him by surprise.'

'Nobody could have surprised Orson.'

Nathaniel licked his lips, hoping that he'd given Clarke enough time to set up whatever surprise he was planning if he had, in fact, feigned his own death.

'Clarke did, by pretending to be dead.' Nathaniel laughed and set his chin high as he relished his next words. 'Just like he did last night.'

Reagan shrugged. Then the implication hit him and horror flared in his eyes before he whirled round to face the law office.

'Hellfire!' he said.

15

'Clarke can't be alive,' Upton said. 'We saw him kill himself.'

'We didn't,' Reagan said. 'He was in the office when we heard the gunshot.'

'We saw all the blood.'

'It didn't have to be his. Lawrence was bleeding everywhere.' Reagan pointed at the doorway. 'And no matter what you say, the body isn't there no longer.'

'That's probably because they moved it.'

When Reagan looked doubtful Upton waved an angry hand at him and then set off, walking purposefully. Despite his comments, when he approached the law office he slowed down and then stopped in front of the doorway. Then, cautiously, he moved on.

The rising sun was casting pale light along the highest points of the pass, but the light in town was still low and the law office interior was dark. Upton stood in front of where they'd left the body and looked around, then with a shrug he slipped inside.

A satisfied mutter sounded, followed a moment later by a pained grunt. A thud followed and then a gunshot.

Everyone outside turned to the door, but long moments passed without Upton emerging. When Reagan swung his gun round to aim at the doorway, Nathaniel backed away for a pace. When neither of the gunmen reacted to him he turned on his heel and leapt at Elmore.

As Reagan had been aiming at Nathaniel, Elmore had aimed his gun at Shackleton, so he took a moment to react. By the time he'd turned Nathaniel was leaping at him.

Nathaniel barged into Elmore's chest knocking him backward for a pace. His earlier tussle with Elmore helped him to judge how his opponent would react, so when Elmore tried to slap his head with his gun, Nathaniel grabbed his wrist and twisted it.

He swung the gun away from his head and then down past his chest making Elmore strain to twist the other way. Then Shackleton moved in on them, seeking to help Nathaniel.

With a grunt of desperation Elmore fired, making a bullet whistle past Nathaniel's hip and causing Shackleton to jerk to one side and then come at Elmore from the other. Nathaniel couldn't see what Reagan was doing, but he put that concern from his mind and twisted Elmore's wrist the other way.

Elmore fired again. Then his eyes widened; when Nathaniel looked down he saw that he'd turned the barrel inwards towards Elmore's side and the bullet had driven into his body.

Elmore slumped. Nathaniel tore the gun from his weakening grasp. Elmore shook himself and made a lunge for the gun. Nathaniel fired a second bullet in his chest.

As Elmore dropped to his knees Nathaniel twisted to face towards where

Reagan had been, but then stopped himself when he saw that Reagan was no longer standing outside the law office.

He backed away from Elmore, letting the man slide lifelessly to the ground, and turned to Shackleton, who shrugged. Both men whirled round on the spot, but in the few moments while Nathaniel had been tussling with Elmore, Reagan had fled.

'I guess he's not the only one who can do the unexpected,' Shackleton said.

'It's three against one now,' Nathaniel answered, raising his voice to ensure Reagan heard them. 'He had no choice but to run.'

'He knows he won't prevail now,' Shackleton called, equally loudly. 'Just like Orson White.'

Nathaniel turned to the law office. 'Is that right, Clarke?'

Long moments passed in silence, making Nathaniel wonder if he might have misunderstood the situation. Then Clarke spoke up from just inside the door.

'The trick worked once before when I was desperate,' he said. 'And I was desperate again.'

Clarke had spoken at the same volume as Nathaniel and Shackleton had used, so, presuming that he was taunting Reagan in the hope that he'd reveal where he'd gone to ground, Nathaniel called the appropriate response.

'What happened the last time?'

'You mostly figured it out. Money was on offer for whoever tamed the town, and Orson decided it was enough for him to turn against the other gunslingers.'

'What happened to the money?'

'I don't know. Orson struck a deal in advance, but I was only interested in taking him down. I don't know where he stashed it.'

'I assume Reagan decided not to take him on?'

'Sure. Anyone who faced Orson down was sure to end up dead. Reagan stayed away from the trouble just as I did. Sure enough, Orson gunned down everyone and then combed the pass for the ones that had fled. Then he returned to the law office, and that was his downfall.'

'You were waiting for him?'

'Yup, just like I did when I waited for Upton. When Orson arrived in town he found me lying apparently dead on the floor. I was still there when he'd finished.'

With no obvious way to continue the taunting Nathaniel gave the town a longer look over. Seeing no sign of where Reagan had gone to ground, he faced Shackleton.

'We split up,' Shackleton whispered. 'You take the other side. I'll cover this side.'

'I have the gun,' Nathaniel said. 'I'll take the risks and you head for cover.'

'You've taken too many risks already, and it's time you remembered I'm in charge.'

Nathaniel conceded Shackleton's point with a nod. As he moved off cautiously, Shackleton hurried to the side of the law office to use the available cover, while Clarke stayed inside the office.

Nathaniel eyed with suspicion the open wagon that Reagan had used and he approached it, craning his neck. The wagon proved to be empty other than for the coffin. Nathaniel leaned over to tap the side, but this caused the coffin to move, confirming that Reagan wasn't hiding inside.

He looked down the wide street. The nearest building was the stable and he judged that this was the only place Reagan could have reached during the short time his attention had been on Elmore.

He walked at an angle to the doorway, passing the body that had been thrown out of the stable last night. At the doorpost he stopped and listened.

When he heard nothing he went inside and quickly jerked to one side to stand with his back to the wall. He could see into all corners and Reagan wasn't here.

It looked increasingly likely that Reagan had holed up on Shackleton's side of town. Nathaniel slipped outside and stood beside the doorpost. Shackleton was making his cautious way across the front of the building next to the law office, so Nathaniel attracted his attention with a wave and then shrugged questioningly.

Shackleton got his meaning: that he was requesting orders; he beckoned him to move on in the same direction as himself. Nathaniel nodded and, walking sideways, he matched Shackleton's slow pace.

He had covered five paces beyond the corner of the stable when something about the scene ahead looked odd, although he couldn't work out what it was. Then he winced.

The body was no longer lying on the ground.

'Clarke's not the only one who can do that trick,' Reagan said from behind him.

Nathaniel whirled round, unsure where the voice had come from, then he jerked his head down in self-preservation. This proved to be the right course of action when a gunshot blasted and he heard the bullet clatter into the stable wall behind him.

He kept his head down and ran for the wagon. It was five paces away and after running three frantic steps he threw himself to the ground and with a scrambling roll over a shoulder he slammed to a halt on his back beneath the wagon.

Reagan hadn't fired again, so Nathaniel assumed he had shot at him over the back of the coffin. He rolled on to his front and looked across the street to where Shackleton was frantically looking around, thereby confirming his assumption.

'Shoot at the wagon, Clarke,' Shackleton shouted. 'Pin Reagan down.'

He looked at the law office, waiting for Clarke to follow his order, but there was no reaction. Shackleton peered at the wagon and then hurried towards the office.

'You heard him, Clarke,' he shouted. 'Start shooting.'

Still Clarke didn't respond, then creaking sounded above Nathaniel as Reagan changed position. Nathaniel couldn't work out where Reagan was and he didn't want to betray his own position by shooting wildly, so he crawled to the back of the wagon.

He slipped round a wheel and knelt down while he waited for Reagan to appear. Long moments passed while Shackleton moved on to the law office door, his face thunderous after Clarke had ignored him.

Shackleton had reached the doorway and was moving to swing himself inside when Reagan fired. The gunshot clattered into the wall inches away from Shackleton's hand, making him drop down.

The firing helped Nathaniel work out Reagan's position at the front of the wagon and he leapt to his feet. As it turned out Reagan was clambering on to the driver's seat. Nathaniel aimed at him.

He fired and his gunshot sliced into

the back of the seat. As he took more careful aim, Reagan snapped his arm to one side and picked him out.

Nathaniel still fired and then dived. Before he hit the ground he heard Reagan's gunshot and saw the brim of his hat kick.

He looked towards Shackleton to see if he'd get a signal that he'd hit his target, but then Reagan leapt down from the seat. He landed with one knee bent and then let his momentum keep him moving until he landed on his side.

Reagan slid across the ground, firing at Nathaniel. The shot sliced into the hardpan to Nathaniel's side and Nathaniel reckoned it had missed him only because Reagan was moving.

Nathaniel resisted the urge to try to scramble to safety again and he followed Reagan. A moment before he fired a gunshot roared out from the law office.

Reagan bucked and then bucked a second time when Nathaniel's shot hammered into his lower chest. Reagan still managed to fire, but the shot wasted itself in the air and by the time he'd lowered his gun to aim at him, Nathaniel was firing again, this time slicing a shot into his upper chest.

Clarke tore out two more shots, but by then Reagan had rolled over on to his back. Nathaniel watched him for a moment, but when Reagan didn't move again, he stood up.

Across the main drag Shackleton nodded to Nathaniel. Then he turned to the law office, from where for the first time Clarke emerged.

'We got him in the end,' Clarke said with a smile.

He held out a hand to help Shackleton to his feet.

'Except you hid while we took the risks,' Shackleton said. He ignored the hand and got to his feet on his own.

Clarke shrugged. 'I'm a survivor. I lived to tell the tale of what happened here five years ago, and I've done it again.'

16

Clarke walked past Shackleton and across the main drag to stand over Reagan's body. He nodded and then turned to Nathaniel, who, feeling unable to thank Clarke for what he'd done, moved away to stand with Shackleton.

'I'm heading back to Lone Pine, so I guess this is where we part company,' Clarke said, facing them. 'And it's just like the last time, with me facing an uncertain future and you heading off on another assignment.'

'I'm not sure we can deem my last assignment to be completed,' Shackleton said.

Clarke shrugged. 'Temple is dead. Your assignment died with him.'

Clarke's lack of concern for Temple's demise made Nathaniel take a long pace forward, his fists bunching. Shackleton slapped a hand on his shoulder and

Nathaniel gave one last lunge forward before he stilled.

Shackleton gave an approving nod and turned to Clarke.

'You're right, but Temple was seeking revenge against the man he thought had killed his son. He was wrong, but as it turned out your actions here five years ago ultimately led to Reagan taking revenge.'

'I'm not to blame for another man's actions, and, either way, I thought you were a man who just did his duty and never got personally involved.'

'I still think that's the best way to deal with my job, but recently I've been forced to wonder whether there might be exceptions.' Shackleton glanced at Nathaniel, who smiled. Then he advanced a long pace on Clarke. 'I reckon you can be the first exception.'

Clarke winced. 'So what are you saying I should do?'

'For the last five years everyone has called you the man who tamed Lone Pine. We need to return to town and let everyone know the truth: that you were only the man who killed the man who tamed Lone Pine.'

'Orson White was a deadly gun-slinger, so it amounts to the same thing.'

'I'm sure it does.' Shackleton flashed a smile. 'So you'll have no problem with telling everyone the truth.'

Clarke shook his head. 'I've made Lone Pine a safe town. Now that Reagan's dead, it'll be a peaceful town again, but news like that will make sure I face plenty of trouble from men who reckon they can take me on now.'

Shackleton snorted a laugh. 'A man who is ruthless enough to let others take the greater risks, determined enough to win through no matter what the odds, and devious enough to play dead, twice, will deal with them.'

'And a man like that has no trouble ignoring your demand.'

When Shackleton didn't respond Clarke snorted and turned away. With a move like lightning Shackleton jerked forward and grabbed Clarke's shoulder.

He spun him round and with a round-armed blow he punched Clarke's cheek, sending him rocking backwards. An uppercut to the chin toppled him.

'You picked the wrong man to ignore,' he muttered.

Clarke glared up at Shackleton, but when Nathaniel stood at his shoulder Clarke got to his feet and raised his hands in a placating gesture.

'All right,' he said. 'Perhaps you're right, and now is the right time for the full story to be known. After all, so much time has passed and so few people are left in Lone Pine from those times I doubt anyone will care.'

With that pronouncement Clarke turned away. Rubbing his jaw, he busied himself with dragging the bodies of the dead men to the wagon.

The other two men watched him in silence until Nathaniel turned to Shackleton.

'I'm sorry this situation lost you a friend,' he said.

'I'm pleased I lost only one friend,' Shackleton replied.

'Sure, and you need to know I only did what I thought was right while Temple only ever wanted to know what happened to his son.'

Shackleton nodded. 'Before he died I reckon we worked out enough of what happened to give him some peace.'

Nathaniel grunted that he agreed and they moved on to join Clarke. There, without asking, Shackleton took Reagan's shoulders and dragged him towards the wagon. Nathaniel busied himself with collecting Temple's body and placing it with the others.

When the bodies were lined up, with Clarke taking each man's legs and Shackleton their shoulders, one by one they lugged them into the back of the wagon. When they'd deposited Elmore's body, Clarke moved round to the front of the wagon; Nathaniel leaned closer to Shackleton.

'Are you sure he'll tell the full truth?' he asked.

'I trust him enough to do that.' Shackleton sighed. 'But if he doesn't, we'll make sure everyone knows what really happened here, both five years ago and today.'

'We will, but I reckon Clarke might have been right. Nobody will care enough to change their opinion of him.'

Shackleton nodded. 'Which is as it should be. No matter if Clarke got his reputation falsely, he's done his duty for the last five years. That matters the most, especially when in a way he is still the man who tamed Lone Pine.'

'In other words, only the result matters, and not what he had to do to get it.'

Shackleton rubbed his jaw as he watched Clarke clamber on to the seat.

'Sure,' he said cautiously.

'Which means there really are times when you have to get personally involved,' Nathaniel mused, 'provided that in the end it all works out for the best.'

'I guess you're right, but you have to

accept this was an exception.' Shackleton pointed a warning finger at Nathaniel. 'It doesn't mean we'll ever get involved again.'

Nathaniel glanced at Shackleton from the corner of his eye.

'If you say so,' he said.

LEGEND OF THE DEAD
MEN'S GOLD
BULLET CATCH SHOWDOWN
ALL MUST DIE
THE MYSTERY OF SILVER FALLS